Six Acres and a Third

*The publisher gratefully acknowledges
the generous contribution to this book provided
by the Literature in Translation Endowment Fund
of the University of California Press Foundation,
which is supported by a major gift
from Joan Palevsky.*

Six Acres and a Third

*The Classic Nineteenth-Century Novel
about Colonial India*

Fakir Mohan Senapati

Translated from Oriya by Rabi Shankar Mishra,
Satya P. Mohanty, Jatindra K. Nayak,
and Paul St-Pierre

UNIVERSITY OF CALIFORNIA PRESS

Berkeley   Los Angeles   London

University of California Press
Berkeley and Los Angeles, California
University of California Press, Ltd.
London, England

© 2005 by The Regents of the University of California

Library of Congress Cataloging-in-Publication Data

Senapati, Fakir Mohan, 1843–1918.
  [Chha Mana Atha Guntha. English]
  Six acres and a third : the classic nineteenth-century novel
about colonial India / [written by] Fakir Mohan Senapati;
translated from Oriya by Rabi Shankar Mishra . . . [et al.].
    p.   cm.
  In English, translated from Oriya.
  Originally published: 1901.
  Includes bibliographical references.
  ISBN 0-520-22882-0 (cloth : alk. paper).—
ISBN 0-520-22883-9 (pbk. : alk. paper)
  I. Mishra, Rabi Shankar.   II. Title.
PK2579.S4C513   2006   2005015750

Manufactured in the United States of America
14 13 12 11 10 09 08 07 06 05
10 9 8 7 6 5 4 3 2 1

Printed on Ecobook 50 containing a minimum 50%
post-consumer waste, processed chlorine free. The balance
contains virgin pulp, including 25% Forest Stewardship
Council Certified for no old-growth tree cutting, processed
either TCF or ECF. The sheet is acid-free and meets the
minimum requirements of ANSI/NISO Z39.48-1992 (R 1997)
(Permanence of Paper).

CONTENTS

Introduction

Satya P. Mohanty

Set in colonial Indian society during the early decades of the nineteenth century, *Six Acres and a Third* tells a tale of wealth and greed, of property and theft. On one level it is the story of an evil landlord, Ramachandra Mangaraj, who exploits poor peasants and uses the new legal system to appropriate the property of others. But this is merely one of the themes in the novel; as the text unfolds it reveals several layers of meaning and implication. Toward the end of Mangaraj's story, he is punished by the law and we hear how the "Judge Sahib" ordered that his landed estate, his "zamindari," be taken away. It is sold to a lawyer, who—as rumor in the village has it—"will come with ten palanquins followed by five horses and two hundred foot soldiers" to take possession of Mangaraj's large estate. The ordinary villagers react to this news by reminding one another of an old saying: "Oh, horse, what difference does it make to you if you are stolen by a thief? You do not get much to eat here; you will not get much to eat there. No matter who becomes the next master, we will remain his slaves. We must look after our own interests."

Fakir Mohan Senapati's novel is written from the perspective of the horse, the ordinary villager, and the foot soldier—in other words, the laboring poor of the world. Although it contains a critique of British colonial rule, the novel offers a powerful indictment of many other forms of social and political authority as well. What makes *Six Acres* unusual is that its critical vision is embodied in its narrative style or mode, in the complex way the novel is narrated and organized as a literary text. The story of Mangaraj and his evil deeds is presented in the narrative as one among many such stories, but the thematic resonances of the other stories and histories can be appreciated only by an attentive reader. Senapati's novel is justly seen as representing the apex of the tradition of literary realism in nineteenth-century Indian literature.[1] But its realism is complex and sophisticated, not simply mimetic; the novel seeks to analyze and explain social reality instead of merely holding up a mirror to it.

In his magisterial *History of Indian Literature, 1800–1910*, Sisir Kumar Das calls Senapati's novel the "culmination of the tradition of realism" in modern Indian literature, referring to its implicit links with earlier instances of realism in fiction and drama. "All these plays and novels contain elements of realism in varying degrees but none can match Fakir Mohan's novel in respect of its minute details of social life and economic undercurrents regulating human relationships and the variety of characters representing traditional occupational groups."[2] Both the naturalist realism that builds on the accumulation of details and the analytical realism I mentioned above, which explains and delves into underlying causes, are achieved in Senapati's novel through a self-reflexive and even self-parodic narrative mode, one that reminds us more of the literary postmodernism of a Salman Rushdie than the naturalistic mode of a Mulk Raj Anand. Central to this narrative mode is a narrator who actively mediates between the reader and the subject of the novel, drawing attention away from the tale to accentuate the way it is told. Until we become comfortable with this narrator and his verbal antics, join him in witty interchange, and ponder our own implication as readers in the making and unmaking of "facts," both narrative and social, we cannot say that we have fully engaged with Senapati's sly and exhilarating text.

Indeed, even the first few lines of the novel invite such an active relationship between narrator and reader. We are given facts that are themselves partial, and at least partly fictional, and it is up to us to interrogate the authority of the teller. As storyteller, the narrator is in fact playing a variety of social roles. As readers, we are encouraged to participate in the decoding of these roles, in inhabiting a dynamic space where social meanings are being constructed and exposed almost simultaneously. The subject is Ramachandra Mangaraj, the hero of our story:

> Ramachandra Mangaraj was a zamindar—a rural landlord—and a prominent moneylender as well, though his transactions in grain far exceeded those in cash. For an area of four kos around, no one else's business had much influence. He was a very pious man indeed: there are twenty-four ekadasis in a year; even if there had been forty such holy days, he would have observed every single one. This is indisputable.

The first two sentences appear to be factual, unlike the next two, which contain the narrator's interpretation. But if you were inclined to dispute the narrator's emphatic conclusion about Mangaraj, or if you had doubts that the observance of ritual fasts may not be conclusive evidence of "piety," you may well begin to wonder why the discussion of Mangaraj's pious nature comes immediately after the two sentences about his property and his money-lending business. The information in the second sentence would then begin to look a little less natural and simple, and you might ask if it was merely an accident that "for . . . four kos around, no one else's business had much influence." Senapati's Indian readers may also have been placed on alert by the obvious exaggeration in the third sentence: an "ekadasi" is the eleventh day of every fifteen-day lunar cycle, and so, by definition, we cannot have forty ekadasis! One way or another, every attentive reader is introduced not so much to the virtues of the landlord Mangaraj as to the unexpected shifts in the narrator's tone. We are asked to be on our toes, to be active interpreters—not simply as literary critics but also as social beings. The Oriya word for moneylender in the text is *mahajana*, literally "noble man"; the link between moneylender and virtue is not the narrator's own creation, but is instead a social and linguistic convention, reflecting a commonly held prejudice encoded in everyday language. What the narrator urges us to do is to question this seemingly natural link. Once we begin to do that the discursive values of Senapati's narrator are a bit easier to grasp and understand.

A key feature of the narrator's discourse is *irony*. Statements do not mean what they seem to say. More generally, actions that seem to be virtuous may need to be interpreted more carefully, for appearance and reality do not always coincide, and the social world may be quite different from the one that is depicted for us by our scribes, our priests, our rulers, and our teachers—those invested with authority. The irony of the narrator can be subtle, but it often swells to full-blown sarcasm, at times evoking an irreverent and explosive form of humor. This wide tonal range is what the narrator draws on to organize our critical and evaluative perspective. Here is the rest of the first paragraph, which marks major shifts in tone that represent only a part of the full tonal range that is used in the novel:

> Every ekadasi [Mangaraj] fasted, taking nothing but water and a few leaves of the sacred basil plant for the entire day. Just the other afternoon, though, Mangaraj's barber, Jaga, let it slip that on the evenings of ekadasis a large pot of milk, some bananas, and a small quantity of khai and nabata are placed in the master's bedroom. Very early the next morning, Jaga removes the empty pot and washes it. Hearing this, some people exchanged knowing looks and chuckled. One blurted out, "Not even the father of Lord Mahadeva can catch a clever fellow stealing a drink when he dips under the water." We're not absolutely sure what was meant by this, but our guess is that these men were slandering Mangaraj. Ignoring their intentions for the moment, we would like to plead his case as follows: Let the eyewitness who has seen Mangaraj emptying the pot come forward, for like judges in a court of law we are absolutely unwilling to accept hearsay and conjecture as evidence. All the more so since science textbooks state unequivocally: "Liquids evaporate." Is milk not a liquid? Why should milk in a zamindar's household defy the laws of science? Besides, there were moles, rats, and bugs in his bedroom. And in whose house can mosquitoes and flies not be found? Like all base creatures of appetite, these are always on the lookout for food; such creatures are not spiritually minded like Mangaraj, who had the benefit of listening to the holy scriptures. It would be a great sin, then, to doubt Mangaraj's piety or unwavering devotion.

Authorities are cited to defend Mangaraj, as in a law court. The aim is to draw attention, through the exaggerated tone, to the wiliness of those who are powerful, who can quote scripture to serve their own ends. But the allusion is not only to the currently dominant colonial legal system, but also to an even more revered authority—the classical Indian discourse the *Nyaya Shastra* (*The Treatise on Logic*), which elaborated a complex system of syllogistic reasoning.[3] The main effect is humor and parody; one authoritative system after another is used, with the stated goal of trouncing Mangaraj's slanderers and enemies. Illegitimate power and authority are exposed through the crucial bits of incriminating information given by the narrator, pleading on behalf of Mangaraj (apparently unwittingly): the report from Jaga the barber, for instance. This is in fact the primary method by which Senapati's satire works. The narrator sets himself up as a witty and loquacious fellow who is seedy because of his motivations; he seems too close to the powerful, and acts like one of their henchmen. But of course that is only what he seems to be doing; in reality, he creates the world of humor, satire, and social criticism that is central to Senapati's vision.

Critics of the novel have not analyzed this narrator adequately, even though everyone notices his ubiquitous presence. In creating the narrator, I would like to argue, Senapati has drawn on an existing social type—the "touter"—in Oriya culture. From the point of view of the middle class, the touter (its etymological connections in Oriya are with both the English *tout* and with *lawyers*, a new profession in late nineteenth-century Oriya society) is the disreputable wit who inhabits the lower rungs of society and is always a bit unreliable (a bit like the Fool in European drama, or the Signifying Monkey in West African traditions).

Senapati transforms this rather unsavory type into a new kind of social agent: in his novel, the touter is the only person who can survive Mangaraj's oppression and chicanery. He does this by using wit and intelligence to disguise his motives, and not only survives, but ends up being an effective social and cultural actor as well. Writing from the vantage point of the downtrodden poor—the horse, the laborer, the peasant—Senapati transforms the disreputable touter of the Oriya middle-class imagination into a self-conscious satirist, social critic, and moral philosopher. The touter-narrator enters the modern Indian novel from the world of oral discourse; his rhythms and shifting moods make him the quintessential satirist who reaches beyond the delicate sensibilities of the middle class to create a new kind of reader and a new kind of self-critical social subject. Senapati's goal is not just to satirize the likes of Mangaraj, the obviously evil landowner, but also to examine his middle- and upper-class Oriya readers, the new babus, seduced by the trappings of the colonizers' culture and distanced from their own.

> At the edge of the weavers' quarter is the Bhagavataghara and the temple to Lord Dadhi Bamana, built from cash contributions raised among the weavers. Do you know how cash contributions are raised? Although you may need no explanation, the new babus do, for they are educated: they have studied and have mastered profundities. Ask a new babu his grandfather's father's name and he will hem and haw, but the names of the ancestors of England's Charles the Third will readily roll off his tongue. To be considered a scholar, it is necessary to have read about the English or the French; there is no point in learning about oneself or one's neighbor. But all this is probably not very important. We should not run the risk of displeasing our babus with such unnecessary remarks.

We shall see later how the narrator's critiques add up to a coherent and systematic social and ethical vision. The seemingly "postmodern" reflexivity of the narrative represents a carefully fashioned narrative, epistemic, and ethical stance toward the various forms of power and authority that colonial modernity produces in Orissa. This stance is based on a new and active relationship between reader and narrator.

As unprepared readers, we face a number of obvious problems. What do we do with a narrator who interrupts his long digressions from his narrative to tell us repeatedly that he does not like to digress? How do we deal with the fact that he quotes approvingly authorities like "the great pundit Benjamin Franklin" for having taught the virtues of economical and prudent use of resources, but often goes on to waste his and our precious time without getting to the point of his story? And what, finally, are we to make of his attempt in chapter 6 to describe Champa, one of the central characters of the story, by pompously invoking (quoting, misquoting, and sometimes deliberately mistranslating) classical Sanskrit writers like Kalidasa and authoritative treatises on poetics like the *Alankar Shashtra*, when we end up getting more literary satire and critical commentary on nineteenth-century literary tastes than a physical description of Champa? As a storyteller, our narrator does not seem very skilled. Chapter 8, for instance, which tells us how Mangaraj acquired his zamindari, seems to waste several paragraphs before introducing Sheikh Dildar Mian, the dissolute landowner from whom Mangaraj gets his estate. It is only in chapter 10, almost halfway into the novel, that we get to meet Bhagia and Saria, and are introduced to their "six and a third acres," after which the main action can begin (it really moves forward only in chapter 13). One solution to all these problems, a possible answer to our questions, is that Senapati's narrator simply has trouble getting directly to the point; perhaps his indirections will help us find the true direction of his tale. The story of Bhagia and Saria's land, of Mangaraj's appropriation of it and of his subsequent fall, may not be as important as the other stories we hear indirectly as the narrator struggles to tell this story. And if we pay attention to some of the information that comes to us indirectly, we may begin to see the story of property, greed, and the wiles of the powerful, in a new light, from a wider historical vantage point, and through the wiser eyes of the horse, the peasant, and the bonded laborer.

After all, the land that Mangaraj acquires by guile from Sheikh Dildar Mian was itself acquired by Mian's father through corrupt means: Ali Mian rose from minor police officer to landlord within a few short years. After the massive upheavals created by the new colonial land-tenure laws, when zamindaris that had lasted for several generations were bought and sold by the deceitful, a new class of predatory social being emerges, and Mangaraj is simply one among many like him.[4] There are indeed many who belong to this social and moral type, and as Mangaraj gets ready to acquire Dildar Mian's property, the narrator has his own quiet dig at the all-powerful East India Company itself, putting its power in historical perspective. Here is how the chapter ends: "Historians say it took Clive less time to get the Bengal Subedari from the emperor of Delhi than it takes one to buy and sell a donkey. How long do you think it will take Mangaraj to get the zamindari of Fatepur Sarsandha from Mian?" This is a seemingly minor allusion, and it digresses, for it is only incidental to the plot, but it is through such digressions and allusions that Senapati builds up a rich metaphorical subtext for his novel.

From the vantage point of the underdog, the poor, the marginal elements of society, many of history's heroes look decidedly unglamorous. If Mangaraj the noble "mahajana" and the famous "Lord" Clive of England's mighty East India Company are indeed close cousins, then it is hard to be seduced by the trappings of the socially powerful. Viewed this way, the main plot of *Six Acres* seems deliberately typical, and the central focus of the novel is not the story of Mangaraj and the poor peasant couple but rather the witty and allusive discourse of the narrator.

One of the underlying concerns of the narrator's discourse is this question: who has social and political power? His parodic and humorous invocation of various forms of authority is not just a form of debunking, for it invites readers to engage in a form of moral inquiry as well. Behind the question about power lies a more radical one: what, if anything, *justifies* power? If social power derives from ownership of property and wealth, which are themselves lost (stolen) as easily as they are won, then both property and power seem insecure possessions, vulnerable to the vagaries of luck and historical accident. Ultimately, these questions lead to the suggestion that *all* property may be theft after all, and the only true owners are those who create social value, the laboring masses. So while Mangaraj's crimes against Bhagia and Saria are real and are morally as well as legally culpable, there is a gentle reminder that even the peasant couple are not natural owners of the plot of land either. Bhagia inherits the land from his father, Gobinda Chandra, as he does the post of paramanika, or headman, of the community of weavers in the village. Gobinda, we are told, is a worthy, highly respected man, one who acquired his cherished plot of land not through deceit but with his own money. When one of the older zamindar families was in decline, portions of their land were sold off cheaply and Gobinda happened to be lucky. But was it just luck? The paramanika is not quite a weaver or farmer; he is a middleman of sorts. Here is how we hear about it:

> Gobinda did not, himself, weave clothes for a living; he collected clothes made by weavers and sold them in the market. Or, if a middleman came to the village, he would arrange to sell clothes to him. In doing so, he made a good profit. People were under the impression that Gobinda had made thousands. But we know that villagers are in the habit of exaggerating their own age and other people's wealth. Nonetheless, it is true that Gobinda did come by some money. When the fortunes of the family of Zamindar Bagha Singh began to decline, pieces of land were sold off. One of these, close by the village of Gobindapur, was purchased by Gobinda. It measured six and a third acres and was rent-free. There is a saying which goes, "A field made fertile by drainage water from a village always ends up in the hands of the village rent collector." In other words, the rent collector gets the best land. The piece of land Gobinda bought was watered by the village drains and so was very fertile. Since water was plentiful, it produced a rich harvest of rabana rice. They say, "If you have good land, plant only rabana; it will grow cubit-long ears, and be the envy of your neighbor." Flood or drought, the land yielded eight bharanas of grain per acre. But, Bhagia was a weaver, what did he know about farming? He gave it out to sharecroppers and received only about five bharanas per acre.

The narrator's tone is gentle, but there is no mistaking the implication of the saying about the rent collector. The ownership of property, Senapati suggests, is due less to merit than to luck and to power and privilege. The moral justification of such ownership is at best very tenuous. The social and political vision underlying *Six Acres and a Third* is thus more radical than its readers have often recognized. True, Senapati tells us about the Khandayats of medieval Orissa, the warriors who were given land in lieu of payment for their services to the state, and we also hear about Brahmins being given rent-free land for similar reasons. This suggests a form of justified ownership of social property, for it is payment for work done for the social good. But the precolonial world of the Khandayats, it is suggested, was organized along lines that are radically different from what exists now. We are given hints of it in the description of generosity and openness of the older Bagha Singh. It suggests a moral economy in which ownership might be considered a form of trusteeship, rather than what it is in the world of Clive, Dildar Mian, and Mangaraj. John Boulton, one of the Senapati's most insightful readers, is thus right to say that what Senapati envisioned as an alternative to Mangaraj's world was a form of "religious socialism," one inspired by *dharma*, or the just moral order, with its basis in *punya*, the merit that is the natural product of virtuous action.[5]

The two themes of power and the ownership of property are basic to the conceptual structure of Senapati's novel, and in turn bring up questions about belief and action. The narrator's almost obsessive invocation of authority, together with his parody of some forms of authoritative discourse, encourages us to be skeptical about what and whom we must believe. Underlying the linguistic play and the self-consciously allusive style of the narrator's discourse is a similar question about justification: what justifies narrative, and ultimately epistemic, authority? If the touter-narrator who pleads Mangaraj's case is not to be believed, who is? If the scriptural and traditional authorities that are cited can be misinterpreted and misused, can we ever be justified in our use of them? Senapati's answer is not an indiscriminate skepticism, however; as we have seen, his vision is that of a radical social critic, and he is more akin to an Enlightenment *philosophe* than to a skeptic who disavows knowledge altogether. The narrator's digressions, as we have seen, often reveal crucial bits of information that allow us to sort fable from fact, and ideological posturing from genuine social virtue. But a good deal of this work is left up to the reader, who is asked to be an active participant in the process of deconstructing social truths and reimagining alternatives to them. Indeed, this activity—this process—of engagement with the social and discursive world around us emerges as an epistemic virtue in the novel. Senapati's satire arouses our anger, as good satire always does, but the narrator's parodic and self-referential discourse unsettles us with the reminder that we need to be actively involved in analyzing and evaluating. Epistemic virtues, like their moral counterparts, need to be exercised; we cannot passively possess them.

I think this is the context in which we need to see the positive characters of this novel, characters like Saantani, Mangaraj's wife, and Mukunda, the loyal and devoted old servant. They can seem like idealized pictures of selflessness and virtue if we do not recognize that they are also associated with another important quality: silence. Both characters speak only a few words in the novel, but they point us to an altogether different—and older—social and moral universe. Their silence is, by implication, not passive since it enacts an active rejection of the frantic garrulity of the world of Mangaraj and the lawyers, the powerful and the unending discourse that seems to serve only them. Saantani and Mukunda, then, are not unlike Shakespeare's Cordelia in their rejection of debased speech; their silence points to an alternate world in which deeds and speech are congruent rather than at odds, where appearance and reality are not so jarringly askew. Rabi Shankar Mishra has pointed out in an astute reading of the novel that Saantani represents not the lost past but a value that can be "an important element in the newly emerging Oriya society under the impact of British colonialism."

> No wonder Saantani does not have a proper name. She is simply Saantani—a generic identity like a "mother"—one who cares for something or somebody. She is the wife of a Saanta, the traditional landlord in an Oriya village who was expected to be not just an owner of land but a moral authority, a kind of friend, philosopher and guide to the villagers. Rama Chandra Mangaraj is not actually a Saanta. He is an usurper to this status and position. Saantani . . . , however, is in the truest sense the wife of a Saanta. In foregrounding the goodness of a social structure through Saantani, Senapati seems to celebrate a mode of empowerment for women.[6]

Other readers of the novel may not agree with Mishra that the figure of Saantani can be seen as empowering for women (in fact, I am not sure I do), but they would misunderstand Saantani if they did not see her in her context, in particular the context of garrulous speech and silence, of pretense and sincerity, that the narrator's rich discourse establishes from the very first page of the novel. Together with the image of the laboring poor who produce social value but are oppressed and exploited, the ideal of quiet virtue that Saantani and Mukunda represent provides genuine insight into the positive vision of Senapati's intriguing novel. *Six Acres and a Third* is not just about the epistemic virtues embodied in unrelenting critique, satire, and skeptical analysis; it also suggests some of the features of an alternative world, one in which human actions can be morally meaningful, where discourse and deed can seek to be adequate to each other.

. . .

I have said that the narrative mode of *Six Acres* enacts and embodies the social and moral vision of the novel. Senapati's "realism" is complex rather than simply mimetic or descriptive, and while it attempts to accurately depict colonial Orissan society, it does not do so by separating form from content, or the specifically literary from the sociopolitical. His literary innovations have social and ideological implications. If we look more closely at how Senapati is actively revising and rewriting one of his predecessors, for instance, we will see something quite important about Senapati's project and about the development of literary realism in the context of colonial Indian society. Senapati's achievement as a realist writer is primarily evident in the way he analyzes the ideological underpinnings of the literary representation of Indian society. He succeeds as a realist because he focuses not only on the "what" of representation and reference but also on the "how"—on the mediating layers that shape our perceptions and judgments about reality. He is thus a realist not only in the literary sense, but also in the social-theoretical sense; he emphasizes social causes and influences, going beneath the surface features to reveal a more self-reflexive concern with ideological distortion and the possibility of objective knowledge.[7]

Senapati's Oriya novel, as we know, is about life in an eastern Indian village. It is historically and socially very specific, however, for it refuses to accept Orientalist images of the timeless Indian village, presenting instead a complex account of social exploitation under colonial rule. But colonial rulers—that is, the British—don't often appear directly in the novel. Instead, what we get is an unsentimental picture of the exploitative relations among Indian (or Oriya) peasants and landlords, the educated intelligentsia and the ordinary Indian (Oriya). One of the key literary models Senapati has in mind is the award-winning novel *Bengal Peasant Life*, written in English by the Reverend Lal Behari Day, a Bengali writer who was also an ordained minister.[8] *Bengal Peasant Life* is one of the earliest examples of literary realism in India, and it is often cited as exerting an influence on Senapati's realist mode, but what is significant is how Senapati rewrites ideological elements of Day's text. Day's novel, as has been pointed out by some critics, is written in what might be called a submissive tone, presenting colorful sociological details about Bengali village life to its colonial readership.[9] Like many realists before him, in India and elsewhere, Day wishes to write in a plain and unvarnished style, rejecting "anything marvellous or wonderful" in favor of the authentic reality of Indian (Bengali) village life. "My great Indian predecessors—the latchet of whose shoes I do not pretend to be worth to unloose—Valmiki, Vyas, and the compilers of the Puranas, have treated of kings with ten heads and twenty arms; of a monkey carrying the sun in his armpit; of demons churning the universal ocean with a mountain for a churn-staff . . . etc. etc." (5–6). Instead, says Day, he will provide a "plain and unvarnished tale of a plain peasant, living in this plain country of Bengal . . . told in a plain manner" (7). This is from the first chapter of *Bengal Peasant Life*, but it must sound familiar to readers of realist novels from just about every literary tradition. What Senapati, who begins writing twenty-five years or so later, seizes on, however, is that while Day's style may be "plain and unvarnished," his representation of the Indian village is anything but "plain"—that is, unmediated or innocent. Writing in Oriya rather than English, in a colloquial and allusive language as opposed to the tame English prose of his predecessor, Senapati is at pains to redefine realism as much more than a plain unadorned representation written in simple language. There is one chapter in particular (chapter 26 in Day's novel) which seems to have been deliberately rewritten by Senapati (chapter 12). In both novels there is a chapter where ordinary village women are bathing at the village pond. We listen in on the conversation among the women, learning of details of their domestic lives. Here is an excerpt from Day's novel, with its unabashed anthropological tone:

> A woman who is rubbing her feet sees another woman preparing to go, and says to her,
> "Sister, why are you going away so soon? You have not to cook; why are you then going so soon?
> "Sister, I shall have to cook to-day. The elder *bou* is not well to-day: she was taken ill last night."
> "But you have not to cook much. You have no feast in your house?"
> "No; no feast, certainly. But my sister has come from Devagrama with her son. And the fisherman has given us a large *rohita*, which must be cooked."
> "Oh! You have guests in your house. And what are you going to cook?"
> "I am going to cook *dal* of *mashkalai*, one *tarkari*, *badi* fried, fish fried, fish with peppercorns, fish with tamarind, and another dish, of which my sister's son is very fond, namely, *amda* with poppy-seed."
> "The everlasting *badi* and poppy-seed. You bania are very fond of these two things. We Brahmans do not like either of them."

The reason why you Brahmans do not like *badis* is that
you do not know how to make them well. If you once taste
our *badi* you will not forget it for seven months. You would
wish to eat it every day. As for poppy-seed, what excellent
curry it makes. . . . [T]hough you are a Brahman, once taste
my *badi. Badi* will not destroy your caste."
    So saying, the banker woman went away with the *kalasi* on
her waist. (121)

Much of Day's novel is written in this embarrassingly turgid style,
where the main goal seems to be to convert the village women into
specimens of this or that caste, this or that subregion of Bengal, so
that the reader may be amused by these cultural details. Senapati
begins with an entirely different premise. For one thing, his ren-
dition of this conversation is indirect, presented not as direct dia-
logue but rather in the narrator's inimitable voice. The humor is
that of the village storyteller reveling in his oral performance.

The gathering at the ghat became very large when the
women came to bathe before cooking their daytime meals.
If there had been a daily newspaper in Gobindapur, its editor
would have had no difficulty gathering stories for his paper;
all he would have had to do was sit at the ghat, paper and
pencil in hand. He would have found out, for instance, what
had been cooked the previous night, at whose house, and
what was going to be cooked there today; who went to sleep
at what time; how many mosquitoes bit whom; who ran
out of salt; who had borrowed oil from whom; how Rama's
mother's young daughter-in-law was a shrew, and how she
talked back to her mother-in-law, although she married only
the other day; when Kamali would go back to her in-laws;
how Saraswati was a nice girl and how her cooking was good,
her manners excellent . . .

The differences don't appear to be dramatic at first, but what soon emerges is that Senapati is trying to reframe the women's discourse through the humorous and *critical* voice of his narrator. Day's narrator presents his account of the Indian village to the English-educated Indian reader as well as the colonial readership in England, and his tone is suitably deferential. His village women are presented through the eyes of a benign tourist or even an anthropologist. Senapati, on the other hand, is writing in Oriya for educated Oriya readers, some of whom will not only know English but will also have been co-opted by colonial values and ideology. Senapati's touter-narrator is a sly, clever, and critical commentator, who mediates between the Oriya villagers he is talking about and the English-educated Oriya middle class who might read his account. His tone is satirical and subversive; he is thus less the teller of a simple story about Oriya peasant life and more a self-conscious, trickster-like critic of colonial relations and attitudes.

> There was only one pond in Gobindapur, and everyone in the village used it. It was fairly large, covering ten to twelve batis, with banks ten to twelve arm-lengths high, and was known as Asura Pond. In the middle once stood sixteen stone pillars, on which lamps were lighted. We are unable to recount the true story of who had it dug, or when. It is said that demons, the Asuras, dug it themselves. That could well be true. Could humans like us dig such an immense pond? Here is a brief history of Asura Pond, as told to us by Ekadusia, the ninety-five-year-old weaver.
>
> The demon Banasura ordered that the pond be dug, but did not pick up shovels and baskets to dig it himself. On his orders, a host of demons came one night and did the work. But when day broke, it had not yet been completed: there

was a gap of twelve to fourteen arm-lengths in the south bank, which had not been filled in. By now, it was morning, and the villagers were already up and about. Where could the demons go? They dug a tunnel connecting the pond to the banks of the River Ganga, escaped through it, bathed in the holy river, and then disappeared. During the Baruni Festival on the Ganga, the holy waters of the river used to gush through the tunnel into the pond. But, as the villagers became sinful, the river no longer did this. English-educated babus, do not be too critical of our local historian, Ekadusia Chandra. If you are, half of what Marshman and Tod have written will not survive the light of scrutiny.

Notice the revision of one of the central norms of realist literary discourse. The legends and religious mythology which Day wanted to banish from his text are brought back in, both by rehabilitating the illiterate village historian Ekadusia Chandra and by questioning the authority of English historians of Indian village life like Tod and Marshman. But the primary object of satire, the object which frames the discourse, is the English-educated babu, who imitates colonial values mindlessly and accepts uncritically its condescending attitudes toward indigenous Indian culture. The irreverent tone of this passage is present throughout the novel, and if we are to analyze the main way that Senapati revises Day's representation of village life in India, we would have to focus primarily on the mediating role of the narrator in framing the object of representation. Day's Orientalist representation of Bengali village women effectively dehistoricizes their lives; his narrator's gaze swerves up from the Indian village to the timeless world where social life is drained of political specificity. The landlord's daughter, for instance, is supposed to remind us of ancient Egypt: "Her head was uncovered; her body covered in every part with ornaments . . . the silver anklets of her feet made a tinkling noise. . . . All eyes were directed towards her. She had no kalasi at her waist, was attended by two maid-servants, and looked as proud as, to compare small things with great, Pharaoh's daughter might have looked when she went to make her ablution in the Nile" (123–24). References to Greece and Egypt, to various classical and contemporary European models, dominate Day's novel, and they provide the ideological frame through which we are asked to view the Indian village of the second half of the nineteenth century. Colonial rule is rarely mentioned, and if it is, it is made to seem utterly natural, never a political issue.

Senapati's narrator, on the other hand, can't seem to keep colonial rule out of his mind. Here he is, talking about the pond, before the women appear.

> There is another equally irrefutable proof to support this contention [that there are fish in the pond]. Look over there! Four kaduakhumpi birds are hopping about like gotipuas, like traditional dancing boys. The birds are happy and excited because they are able to spear and eat the little fish that live in the mud. Some might remark that these birds are so cruel, so wicked, that they get pleasure from spearing and eating creatures smaller than themselves! What can we say? You may describe the kaduakhumpi birds as cruel, wicked, satanic, or whatever else you like; the birds will never file a defamation suit against you. But don't you know that among your fellow human beings, the bravery, honor, respectability, indeed, the attractiveness of an individual all depend upon the number of necks he can wring?
>   Some sixteen to twenty cranes, white and brown, churn the mud like lowly farmhands, from morning till night. This is the third proof that there are fish in the pond. A pair of kingfishers suddenly arrive out of nowhere, dive into the

water a couple of times, stuff themselves with food, and swiftly fly away. Sitting on the bank, a lone kingfisher suns itself, wings spread like the gown of a memsahib. Oh, stupid Hindu cranes, look at these English kingfishers, who arrive out of nowhere with empty pockets, fill themselves with all manner of fish from the pond, and then fly away. You nest in the banyan tree near the pond, but after churning the mud and water all day long, all you get are a few miserable small fish. You are living in critical times now; more and more kingfishers will swoop down on the pond and carry off the best fish. You have no hope, no future, unless you go abroad and learn how to swim in the ocean.

Reading Lal Behari Day and Fakir Mohan Senapati together in this way, we are faced with the question: do their novels (at least in these two chapters, which so closely resemble each other) refer to a common social reality? Is their referent "village life in India"? Perhaps, but that would be a very partial explanation. For Senapati's novel historicizes and politicizes Day's kind of descriptive realist discourse by drawing attention to the crucial role of the narrative's mediating values and attitudes. We might say that Senapati's discourse, in resituating Day's account of village life in contemporary colonial relations, improves it; it provides a fuller, more objective, and less ideological access to the epistemic object of both novels: village life in colonial Indian society. Understood in this way, we notice the referential continuity between the two novels, but we see that only if we refocus our attention by considering the mediating role of the narrator. After reading Senapati's novel, we cannot see Day as simply writing about nineteenth-century Indian (or Bengali) village women. We see, instead, another common referent emerge, which can be defined more broadly and more specifically as *colonial relations, both literary and ideological.* The object of representation, very narrowly speaking, may be the Indian village women bathing at the pond, but any reader who focuses on that alone will miss the substance of much of what is going on in these novels.

At crucial moments in literary and cultural history, such as the instance I have described here, we can point to *advances* in the referential function of literature. Such advances are not, however, purely literary ones; they cannot be defined narrowly in linguistic or formal terms. Senapati's critique of Day's account of Indian peasants is a critique of ideology, of the ideology that inheres in our representational habits. Given the analytical values and critical attitudes he presents, Senapati's loquacious and wily narrator embodies an epistemic achievement, not just a literary one. It would not be inaccurate to say that this narrator is Senapati's (and the early Indian novel's) contribution to an anticolonial and demystificatory social thought.

. . .

Fakir Mohan Senapati (1843–1918) lived during tumultuous times. Orissa was taken over by the British in 1803, and was soon thereafter incorporated into a transnational economic system. Village life was changed profoundly by the colonial system of rent acquisition, which installed a new relationship between the traditional landlord class and the peasantry. Over the course of the nineteenth century, most of the zamindaris of Orissa were bought—often through deceit—by non-Oriya middlemen who had greater access to the courts and offices of Calcutta, the headquarters of the colonial bureaucracy. Absentee landlordism always produces its own problems, and these problems were compounded by the fact that some traditional forms of manufacture in the cities were abolished by the British. Senapati grew up in the northern Orissan city of Balasore, which had been a thriving port and commercial center built around shipping and the manufacture of salt. After salt manufacture was turned into a monopoly by the British, Balasore's fortunes declined rapidly. In his autobiography, Senapati writes movingly about this:

> As a port and business centre, Balasore had achieved fame in both India and Europe. European merchants from Holland, Denmark, France, and Britain had established trading posts there before moving on to Bengal. But no one's fortunes run smooth forever: ups and downs are a Law of Nature. From time immemorial, the quaysides of Balasore had bustled with people by the thousand. Yet look at them now, silent, desolate, overgrown with wild bushes and as hushed as the cemetery. Even the river has silted up. The whole of Balasore's business in now in the hands of non-Oriyas.[10]

Equally devastating to Oriya society and culture was the colonial government's division of the province into three separate sections, each incorporated into an existing administrative unit. Oriya-speaking populations became a linguistic minority in these larger units, and as a result the cultural infrastructure of both urban and rural Orissa—modern schools, the publishing industry, an educated class of readers and writers—remained inadequately developed. Moreover, there were major crises as well; Senapati spent his early years as a teacher and intellectual organizing others to save the Oriya language from being replaced by Bengali in the Balasore school system! Many middle-class Bengalis would have profited from such an arrangement, and there had been an obviously self-serving move by a small but well-organized group to impose Bengali in schools in Orissa in the 1860s (this had been done in the neighboring province of Assam, where the native Assamese had been replaced by Bengali through government decree).[11]

Senapati's consciousness of being an Oriya developed in this politicized context, where an Oriya cultural identity (like many other minority identities in history) was at risk of disappearing. He did not see himself as primarily a literary figure; indeed, he did not really begin his career as a writer until late in life, when he had retired from teaching and his various administrative positions all over the state. What drove him was less a desire for literary fame than the need to save and protect the language of the people around him. There was a measure of idealism that inspired him, no doubt, but Senapati had a very clear idea of the strategic interests of the various groups at stake. He understood that the future of at least the Oriya middle class was bleak if Bengali instead of Oriya became the official medium of communication in Orissa: educated Oriyas—who had learned Persian, the earlier language of the courts—were going to lose even the few jobs that existed in their towns and cities. The jobs themselves were petty ones—those of a clerk or a school teacher— but on them depended the fate of an entire generation of Oriyas, and indeed of much of Orissan society. Senapati's concern with language as a social force—its seductive power, its authority, its abuses—clearly grew out of the struggles into which he had been thrust early in his life, the struggles to defend and save a language and a culture. The linguistic innovations of *Six Acres and a Third*, Senapati's first novel, need to be appreciated in this wider context. These innovations changed Oriya literature forever and inaugurated the age of modern Oriya prose, but they are based in a vision of social equality and cultural self-determination. It is no surprise that the struggle to save the Oriya language, which produced a larger movement we now call Oriya "nationalism," produced a literary renaissance. Senapati, who was one of the leaders of this cultural movement, was no romantic nationalist, however. His conception of language was based on his progressive social vision. In his prose works, he sought to popularize an egalitarian literary medium that was sensitive enough to draw on the rich idioms of ordinary Oriyas, the language of the paddy fields and the village markets. If he saw the imposition of other languages like Persian, English, or Bengali on Oriyas as a form of linguistic colonialism, it is because he considered the interests of Oriyas—much like the interests of any linguistic community— to be tied to democratic cultural and social access to power. Such access, he thought, was impeded by the artificial authority that was granted to some languages, and to some linguistic forms within a given language.

One example is Sanskrit. Through its allusive and parodic style, *Six Acres* draws attention to the power of Sanskrit, with its authority as the language of scripture and tradition, to impose arbitrary social values. Senapati's Oriya prose uses Sanskrit quite liberally, both directly, in quotations that are then analyzed (and often openly bowdlerized), and indirectly, through a Sanskritized Oriya, to suggest an artificial elevation of tone and sentiment. Such artificiality, Senapati knew, was often the basis of an upper-caste "scholarly" approach to the Oriya language itself. He writes in his autobiography of the local schoolteacher in Balasore, a pundit named Harekrushna Panigrahi, whose "teaching method" consisted in translating ordinary Oriya phrases and sentences into more elevated Sanskritized diction. Thus, "One day a crow sat on the branch of a tree holding a piece of meat in its beak" was taught to the schoolchildren in the following way: "One day, or in the course of one diurnal time-span, a crow, or a corvine avis, sat or became sedent, on a branch or a ramus, of a tree or arbor, holding or supporting, a piece of meat or a segment of animal matter or orifice" (16). The Latinate phrases in Boulton's translation indicate the awkwardness of the schoolteacher's translation of everyday Oriya into a tortuous Sanskritized diction. What Senapati was appalled by was the power such pompous imitation had in the existing educational system. The pomposity reflected class power as well as the pretense of learning, and Senapati's ire was directed against both. The Oriya prose he fashioned in his short stories, essays, and novels was the language of ordinary people, used for everyday communication, for creative interchange rather than the blind imitation of cultural authority. It was a language divested of the trappings of privilege and power, of the sedimented effects of social inequality. It was the natural vehicle for the radical social and political vision of *Six Acres and a Third*.

. . .

Fakir Mohan Senapati was born to a family of some distinction, but the family's fortunes had declined by the time of his birth. The young Senapati was orphaned at an early age; his grandmother, who brought him up, lost most of the family property, and so they were dirt-poor. Senapati taught himself to read and write, and eventually became a highly respected scholar in several languages. He helped John Beames, the British official in Balasore, with his research on a comparative study of Oriya, Bengali, and Assamese, and went on to serve as an administrator under several of the minor kings in the outlying areas of Orissa. He was intellectually restless and adventurous, and had the mind and temper of an inventor. Whether in his linguistic experiments or in his projects to introduce new vegetables to the rural countryside, he had the spirit of a reformer more than that of a writer in search of literary fame. He grew up in a part of colonial India that barely registered in the consciousness of the viceroys and their officials. But it is from this particular vantage point that he created a unique synthesis of the traditional and the contemporary, a synthesis whose power and example are relevant even today.

Perhaps they are relevant *especially* today, when the lure of religious chauvinism and romantic nationalism seem to obscure the need for critique—the critique of inequality, of dogma, of deep-seated social prejudice. These were Senapati's targets, and in order to attack them, he chose to fashion a voice that was both protean and self-reflexive. As we have seen, however, his critique was never merely negative. It was based on a vision of human equality and cultural diversity, of a radical humanism that was fed by a variety of religious traditions.

Fakir Mohan Senapati was born Braja Mohan Senapati, which is a traditional Hindu name. In his autobiography he tells the story of how he came to acquire an Islamic name like Fakir. As a child, he had fallen so ill that his devout grandmother feared that she would lose him. After praying to "every Hindu God and Goddess under the sun," writes Fakir Mohan, she turned to two Muslim pirs, or saints, who lived in Balasore. She promised to give him up to their religious order as a fakir (wandering holy man) if he recovered. He recovered, but then the doting grandmother could not bear to give up her young grandson. So she struck a deal with the saints: she would change Braja Mohan's name to Fakir Mohan and give him up "symbolically": "For the eight days of [the Muslim holy days of] the Muharram each year . . . I [had] to dress up as a fakir in knee-breeches, a high-necked, multi-coloured coat, and a Muslim cap, with a variegated bag hung on my shoulder and a red-lacquered cane held in my hand. Thus attired and my face smeared in pure chalk I would roam through the village morning and afternoon begging from house to house, and in the evening I sold whatever rice I had collected and sent the money to the saints for their offerings" (*My Times*, 6).

It isn't hard to imagine the child Braja Mohan, in the process of becoming Fakir Mohan, reveling in the new role he is asked to play. Masks and disguises are wondrous things, especially to a child, and perhaps the young boy was beginning to feel the sense of power that we get from changing roles, from transforming what seems to be natural and immutable. It is certainly this power that informs the rich explorations of Senapati's marvelous first novel. It is a novel that sees the whole world as acting out its assigned roles, roles that can nonetheless be rewritten even as they are being enacted. As we read *Six Acres and a Third*, we trace the steps of the young child who is still out, wandering from house to house in the village, dressed up as a fakir, daring to see the world with new eyes.[12]

NOTES

1. The Oriya title of Senapati's first novel is *Chha Mana Atha Guntha*, serialized in 1897–99 and published as a book in 1902. He went on to write over twenty short stories and three other novels, some of which

have been damaged through the merciless editing of his son. *Chha Mana* is, however, a much better novel than the other three.

2. Sisir Kumar Das, *A History of Indian Literature, 1800–1910* (New Delhi: Sahitya Akademi, 1991), p. 296.

3. The *Nyaya* tradition is one of the six orthodox schools of Indian philosophy, and can be traced back to the sage Gautama, who lived in the fourth or fifth century B.C.

4. "During those days," as the narrator tells us, "the zamindaris of Orissa were auctioned off in Calcutta."

5. John Boulton, *Phakiramohana Senapati: His Life and Prose-Fiction* (Bhubaneswar: Orissa Sahitya Akademi, 1993).

6. Rabi Shankar Mishra, "The Language of Power and the Silences of a Woman," in *Early Novels in India*, ed. Meenakshi Mukherjee (New Delhi: Sahitya Akademi, 2002), p. 260.

7. The analysis that follows is developed more fully in my article "The Dynamics of Literary Reference: Narrative Discourse and Social Ideology in Two Nineteenth-Century Indian Novels," in *Thematology: Literary Studies in India*, ed. Sibaji Bandyopadhyay (Calcutta: Jadavpur University, 2004), 230–48.

8. Lal Behari Day, *Bengal Peasant Life*, ed. Mahadevprasad Saha (Calcutta: Editions Indian, 1969).

9. See the essay by H. S. Mohapatra and J. K. Nayak, "Writing Peasant Life in Colonial India," *Toronto Review of Contemporary Writing Abroad* (Spring 1996): 29–40.

10. *My Times and I*, trans. John Boulton (Bhubaneswar: Orissa Sahitya Akademi, 1985), p. 15.

11. For Senapati's account of this phase of Orissa's history, see Senapati, *My Times and I*; a comparative analysis of the attempt to impose Bengali on Assam and Orissa, and of the "cultural chauvinism" that accompanied it, can be found in Sudhir Chandra, *The Oppressive Present: Literature and Social Consciousness in Colonial India* (New Delhi: Oxford University Press, 1992), pp. 144–54; for an interesting aside on the phenomenon of cultural chauvinism in Bengal, see especially p. 147. A fuller account of Orissan resistance to the imposition of Bengali—a resistance that was championed by many Orissans of Bengali origin—and of the rise of what is called "Oriya nationalism,"

see Nivedita Mohanty, *Oriya Nationalism: Quest for a United Orissa, 1866–1936* (New Delhi: Manohar, 1982), and Bishnu Narayan Mohapatra, "The Politics of Oriya Nationalism, 1903–1936 (Ph.D. diss., Oxford University, 1990). This general phenomenon—linguistic and cultural chauvinism, as well as the forms of "regional" or "nationalist" resistance to them—is seriously understudied, especially by progressive scholars. An adequate study will need to be comparative, focusing on the entire eastern and northeastern region, and it will need to include the kind of illuminating socioeconomic and ideological analysis offered by Joya Chatterji, in *Bengal Divided: Hindu Communalism and Partition,1932–1947* (Cambridge: Cambridge University Press, 1994); see especially chap. 3, which focuses in part on the nineteenth century ("The Construction of Bhadralok Communal Identity: Culture and Communalism in Bengal," pp. 150–90).

12 My reading of the novel grows out my engagement with the pioneering work of the eminent Oriya scholar Natabara Samantray, whose books and essays have not yet been translated into English. Both John Boulton and Rabi Shankar Mishra (see notes 5 and 6) provide good introductions to Senapati; Mishra's interpretations of the novel in his various essays (in English and Oriya) are among the most innovative and convincing. For an excellent account of the novel through the lens of translation practice and theory, see Paul St-Pierre, "Translating (into) the Language of the Colonizers," in *Changing the Terms*, ed. Sherry Simon and Paul St-Pierre (Ottawa: Ottawa University Press, 2000), pp. 261–88; and "Translating Cultural Difference: Fakir Mohan Senapati's *Chha Mana Atha Guntha*," *META* 42, no. 2 (1997): 423–38.

Six Acres and a Third

. . .

Fakir Mohan Senapati

CHAPTER ONE

Ramachandra Mangaraj

Ramachandra Mangaraj was a zamindar—a rural landlord—
and a prominent moneylender as well, though his transactions
in grain far exceeded those in cash. For an area of four kos
around, no one else's business had much influence. He was a
very pious man indeed: there are twenty-four ekadasis in a year;
even if there had been forty such holy days, he would have observed every single one. This is indisputable. Every ekadasi he
fasted, taking nothing but water and a few leaves of the sacred
basil plant for the entire day. Just the other afternoon, though,
Mangaraj's barber, Jaga, let it slip that on the evenings of ekadasis a large pot of milk, some bananas, and a small quantity of
khai and nabata are placed in the master's bedroom. Very early
the next morning, Jaga removes the empty pot and washes it.
Hearing this, some people exchanged knowing looks and
chuckled. One blurted out, "Not even the father of Lord Mahadeva can catch a clever fellow stealing a drink when he dips

under the water." We're not absolutely sure what was meant by this, but our guess is that these men were slandering Mangaraj. Ignoring their intentions for the moment, we would like to plead his case as follows: Let the eyewitness who has seen Mangaraj emptying the pot come forward, for like judges in a court of law we are absolutely unwilling to accept hearsay and conjecture as evidence. All the more so since science textbooks state unequivocally: "Liquids evaporate." Is milk not a liquid? Why should milk in a zamindar's household defy the laws of science? Besides, there were moles, rats, and bugs in his bedroom. And in whose house can mosquitoes and flies not be found? Like all base creatures of appetite, these are always on the lookout for food; such creatures are not spiritually minded like Mangaraj, who had the benefit of listening to the holy scriptures. It would be a great sin, then, to doubt Mangaraj's piety or unwavering devotion.

Moreover, the law of evidence requires that judges take circumstantial evidence into account. Mangaraj's piety was such that he would not touch even parboiled rice, let alone fresh or salted fish. On dwadasis, the days following ekadasis, he never broke the previous day's fast before feeding the Brahmins. To ensure a regular supply of food for this, Mangaraj, in his great wisdom, had given one acre of land to a grain dealer and another to a sweetmeat seller. On the morning of dwadasi the grain dealer would deliver rice flakes and the sweetmeat seller jaggery, and Mangaraj would invite all twenty-seven Brahmin families in the village of Gobindapur for the ritual feast. Before midday, the business of feeding them was over. Mangaraj himself served them. Putting some rice flakes and a little jaggery on their leaf plates, he would respectfully join his hands and loudly address them: "O exalted ones, be so kind as to express your needs should your require anything more. There is plenty of jaggery, there are plenty of rice flakes; but I know your eyes are big and your stomachs small; and I am sure you have already eaten your fill."

After this, if some greedy Brahmin shamelessly asked for more, the zamindar would delicately pick up a few flakes between two fingers and flick them onto his leaf-plate. When they had finished, the Brahmins would belch heartily, and exclaim, "We are content!" blessing Mangaraj as they rose from their places. The feast finished, Mangaraj would devote himself with great humility to the large amounts of leftover food.

Dear reader, you might well ask, "How was it possible to feed twenty-seven Brahmins with a few rice flakes and a little jaggery?" Well, the Lord works in mysterious ways, my brother, in truly mysterious ways. If we seek answers to such questions, our narrative will grind to a halt. After all, did Jesus Christ not feed twelve hundred of his flock with only two loaves of bread? And even those two loaves were not finished—four baskets of bread were left over. In the forest of Kamyaka, was Lord Krishna not able to feed twelve thousand disciples of the sage Durbasa with a few leaves of spinach? If you have no faith in the powers of great souls such as these, how can we hope to interest you in our re-counting of the Life of Ramachandra Mangaraj?

It has come to our attention that Mangaraj's cousin, Shyam Malla, once made a trip into town, fell in with bad company, and polluted himself by eating cabbage that had been cooked with onions. Iniquities cannot be hidden for very long, and the inci-

dent soon became known to Mangaraj. Had he not come to his
cousin's rescue, Shyam's face would even now be covered with
ugly stubble, a mark of penance. Out of sheer generosity,
Mangaraj made sure the ritual of expiation involved very little expense—a mere fifteen acres of Shyam's rent-free ancestral property. A few days later, Mangaraj summoned Shyam and, speaking
as a family elder, reprimanded him: "Look Shyam, from now on
you should be more careful. Because I was around, people were
there to help you out; otherwise your only option would have
been to convert to Christianity—you and all your ancestors
would have been consigned forever to deepest hell. What's more,
anyone else would have paid you only two rupees per acre,
whereas I gave you five. You are, after all, my cousin; how could
I abandon you? But somehow I feel people only need me when
times are rough; when the going is good, no one spares me even
a thought. Do you remember how you were nowhere to be found
when I needed someone to testify in the criminal case against
Bhima Gauda?"

It is no surprise that the descendants of the wretches who
crucified Christ, and had Goddess Sita banished to the forest,
are now busy slandering the kind and pious Mangaraj. We are
forced, very much against our will, to repeat what these slanderers have to say: that his cousin, whose property had so far been
spared, finally fell into his trap, and that to feed the Brahmins
for having eaten onion, Shyam was forced to sell his land to
Mangaraj. These same people add that the women in Mangaraj's
very own household regularly send Champa to get onions from
the market. Now, for the sake of argument, let us suppose that
Champa does indeed buy onions at the market. Do we have any

proof that anyone eats them? True, according to the Laws of Manu, eating onions is wrong, but where in the scriptures is purchasing them prohibited?* These critics are sullying the reputation of the women of a respectable family. We simply refuse to respond to such charges.

---

*Eating onions is wrong: Citing Manu, whose tenth-century "Laws" codified ethical practices and rituals, including conservative caste-based behavior, for traditional Hindus. The argument playfully mimics the syllogistic reasoning of the *Nyaya Shastra*, and parodies legal arguments, pointing to a theme that runs through this chapter and throughout the novel. (Footnotes in the novel were prepared by Rabi Shankar Mishra and Satya P. Mohanty.)

CHAPTER TWO

A Self-Made Man

A poor man's son, the story goes, Mangaraj was orphaned at the age of seven. His father was so poor there was not enough money to pay for his funeral rites. Nor was there enough for new straw to thatch the roof, and so the walls of the house collapsed. Mangaraj's childhood, his education, his entry into the real world, were full of strange and wondrous happenings. Indeed, the life of a truly great man is never without miracles. To recount them all would take a lot of paper and a lot of time, and we have learned the importance of thrift from no less a teacher than our Mangaraj himself. We follow here a principle of economics laid down by the great pundit Benjamin Franklin, which we interpret thus: it is easier to buy paper from the market than to put it to proper use. In telling our story, we will therefore be guided by the economic principles of Mangaraj, and highlight only the most valuable and salient points.

Mangaraj's landholding, his zamindari, was known as Fatepur Sarsandha. It comprised 28 batis—560 acres—of land guaranteed rent-free, and 15 batis plus 27 scattered acres—327 acres total—of taxable, forfeited land. Of these 27 scattered acres, ownership of 7 was still in dispute before the courts. The zamindari was assessed at five thousand rupees a year.*

Some say Mangaraj had given out, on loan, no less than forty to fifty thousand rupees in cash. But then to ordinary folk, important people seem larger than life. Our best estimate is that these transactions did not exceed fifteen thousand rupees. It goes against our principles to tell lies, and our estimate is based on information supplied by a peon in the Income Tax Department. As for loans of grain, the papers have not been sorted for the last twenty years and we are unable to put an exact figure on them. From the accounts submitted by the man in charge of the granary, however, it is known that Mangaraj collected more than two thousand maunds of rice last year.

Mangaraj's house had five large wings. His three sons occupied three of these, and he, his wife, and their youngest daughter, Malati, lived in another. The outermost wing was the kacheri, his office, whose roof was supported by five large wooden beams, on which were carved images of tigers, elephants, cats, the divine couple Radha and Krishna, and monkeys. On the walls were pictures of lotus and kusuma flowers, garlands of malati flowers, and the events of the legendary battle between Rama and Ravana, with their armies of monkeys and demons—all painted in vivid blues, whites, reds, yellows, and browns. Somewhere in Rajas-

---

Rent-free land: Land was traditionally given by the king as a form of payment or reward for exceptional service (see chapters 3 and 15). Local landlords could not charge rent for such land for generations, and hence it the most attractive land for someone else to acquire through foul means (see chapters 8 and 15, and the introduction).

than, on seeing an image of a nude woman, Tod Sahib came to the conclusion that all women in ancient India went about naked. We could have dispelled the Sahib's ignorance by showing him these pictures on Mangaraj's wall. The fair-skinned goddess Radha, wearing a black dotted skirt, surrounded by her similarly dressed companions, would have been enough to cure the Sahib's ignorance and error. To paint these pictures, it had not been necessary to bring in an artist from another land; our Champa had done all this fine work herself. And she was a rare kind of artist indeed: the animals and birds she painted are not to be found in any ordinary zoo, such as the one in Calcutta.

Just behind Mangaraj's house, there was a large orchard opening onto a big pond, with coconut trees planted all around its edge, and banana, jack-fruit, mango, and ou trees further behind. A fence of young bamboo surrounded the orchard like a fortress wall. Few people are as selfless and altruistic as Mangaraj: even the market in Gobindapur owed its existence and prosperity to him. Without his orchard's bounty of fruits and vegetables—coconuts, bananas, brinjals, pumpkins, green chilies, and so on—the market would have presented a much sorrier sight. Nor was anyone allowed to put his vegetables up for sale until the produce from the zamindar's orchard had all been sold. That was of course as it should be. Would it have been fair to sell inferior goods before high-quality produce? Besides, the market belonged to the zamindar, and the gifts of pumpkins, brinjals, and bananas he received on festive occasions, such as the Oriya New Year, all went straight to the market.

It is recounted that after the construction of the Great Wall of China had been completed, the emperor rounded up all the history writers and put them to death, lest they should leave behind a record of the expenses incurred—for which act we consider the emperor a self-effacing man. Great souls do not go about saying how much money they have spent on a noble deed. For instance, if you asked Mangaraj the cost of building his house, he would exclaim, "Oh, a lot of money, I was ruined!"

Our readers should not become disheartened or grow restive. Such matters are best left to historians and archeologists, who provide accurate information on all things ancient. Nine hundred years after the Puri temple was built, a Sahib was able to figure out exactly how much money had been spent on its construction. If documents exist recording the sales of vegetables from Mangaraj's orchard, can it be that difficult to locate records indicating how much was spent on his house? No one in India performed a funeral on a grander scale than did Dewan Ganga Gobind Singh when his mother passed away. The governor-general instructed the collector of the district to send rice, dal, flour, oil, ghee, coconuts, and bananas free of cost to the dewan. When the Raja of Nabadwipa, Sibachandra, wanted to perform the last rites of his mother in a similar style and requested the dewan to send him the list of expenses, Dewan Ganga Gobind mentioned only the expenses incurred for peripheral items such as cannabis, opium, and tobacco, expecting the raja to arrive from this at an idea of the total expenditure involved. A sum of seventy-two thousand rupees was spent on the funeral, not taking into account the free labor and provisions supplied by local zamindars. We are going to give a similar sort of account of the expenditure for the construction of Mangaraj's house; intelligent readers will be able to draw their own conclusions from the following figures, obtained from the account books. The records of the granary are the only available source of accurate information on the cost of the construction, and these tell us that fifteen bharanas and twenty-two noutis of rice were given out as provisions for the bonded laborers who built the house.

On several occasions we have heard Mangaraj say that he loaned out money and grain only because he could not bear to see others suffer, that he made no profit at all from these transactions. We would maintain that, in fact, the business involved considerable losses for him. After all, not much profit is to be made by lending grain at 50 percent interest. Not just that; whereas he lent out old husked grain, he took in only new juicy grain in return. Dear reader, if you have ever compared the weights of dry and wet clothes you can easily understand Mangaraj's situation. On last year's accounts the bookkeeper had written off the sum of eight rupees and six annas. He was taken to task for forgiving such a huge amount. A summary of the bookkeeper's explanation is as follows: Bhikari Panda took a loan of five rupees. The compound interest on this comes to twelve rupees five annas and eleven paise. The amount collected from Bhikari Panda was seventeen rupees five annas. The remainder was written off.

CHAPTER THREE

Vāṇijye Vasate Lakṣmīs Tadardham Kṛṣikarmaṇi

Commerce makes you rich;
Agriculture does too, though somewhat less so.*

These must be the words of an old-fashioned bard, since a contemporary poet would say, "Commerce makes you rich; a bachelor's degree in law does too, though somewhat less so." Some naive types might mistake Mangaraj's house for that of a lawyer holding a law degree and think sixty-two families must have been impoverished to raise a house so big. But fate, as you know, determines everything. The turbaned lawyer you see lounging in the courthouse corridors can ruin a mere twenty-five families. The zamindar boasted he needed no one's help; he had made the earth yield gold through his own efforts, through the sheer force

*The translation is accurate but Senapati's point is to introduce, in the next sentence, the critique of the newly popular legal profession.

of his will and his God-given intelligence. According to rumor—indeed we know it to be the truth—our Mangaraj, when he began as a humble sharecropper, received only two acres of land from the village headman. Now he had eighty-six acres under his own plough, and about another sixty given out to sharecroppers. He paid very little on this property, most of it being either rent-free or forfeited by poor Brahmins and only partially taxable. He had fifteen pairs of bullocks and, to look after the fields and orchards, twelve farmhands, all untouchables—Bauris, and three Panas. Mangaraj had infused into them the spirit of hard work and a sense of dedication. Health manuals advise us to get out of bed before dawn, and Mangaraj followed this advice to the letter.

The Shastras say: "All rivers run to the sea, where they lose their sweetness and become salty." How right that is! In the same way, wives and servants lose themselves in their master. We have come to know the truth of this by observing Mangaraj's servants. Every day, he would rise before dawn and brush his teeth. Then, from the verandah, he would call out to the farmhands in a loud voice. Just like the cannon shot marking the beginning and close of day in Calcutta, this would rouse the villagers from their sleep and set the young daughters-in-law to their household chores.

The villagers had never been able to fathom the mystery of clocks. All they knew was that when the sun reached the middle of the sky, it was time to unyoke the bullocks. At about the same time every day, farmers working in the fields would watch for Mangaraj's big palm-leaf umbrella to appear from behind the ridges. Mangaraj treated his farmhands like his own children. Now, parents are never satisfied unless they personally make sure their children have eaten their fill. So as soon as his farmhands sat down in a row for their midday meal, the zamindar would call out: "Cook, bring the rice gruel. Hurry up. My boys are dying of thirst." As he had done many times in the past, the cook would then serve two large bowls of the watery liquid to each one. And if a farmhand ever resented having to drink so much gruel before the meal, Mangaraj would deliver a long lecture on its beneficial effects and health-giving properties, persuading them to drink it up. Only after that would he arrange for rice to be served, and then go for his bath.

There were seventeen drumstick trees in the master's orchard, and their leaves possessed certain medicinal properties. They aided digestion, were nourishing and delicious; besides, they helped restore the sick to health. We do not know if books really claim such properties for the leaves of the drumstick tree, but then we have no expertise in that field. We have merely written down what we have heard from Mangaraj himself. Naturally enough, not a single leaf found its way to the market; they were reserved exclusively for the nourishment and well-being of the farmhands. And the flowers of these trees, in Mangaraj's view, constituted the most wholesome food in the world; when cooked with mustard, they were wonderful. In God's creation, good and bad are everywhere intertwined. Consider how a jack-fruit is sweet and wholesome, while its fibers harm the stomach. People who are wise, however, can effortlessly sort the good from the bad. They know that everything the drumstick tree produces is good, except, of course, the drumsticks themselves. Which is why Mangaraj never served those to the farmhands; they went straight to the market.

CHAPTER FOUR

Inspecting the Paddy Field

Ayaṃ nijaḥ paro veti gaṇanā laghucetasām.*

Our Mangaraj was never one to discriminate between his own property and that of others. According to the Shastras, only the small-minded make a distinction between mine and thine. Thus the zamindar gave almost as much attention to his own fields as he did to those belonging to others. For our wise readers, it will suffice to recount just one incident: after all, to know if rice is cooked, you needn't press more than a single grain between your fingers.

One morning the head farmhand, Gobinda Puhan, came to the zamindar and said, "Master, only an acre and a half remain to be planted, but we don't have any more seedlings." Mangaraj lis-

---

*A traditional saying, used ironically: "Only a mean man distinguishes between self and the other."

tened to him and remained silent for a while; the farmhand stood waiting in the courtyard, his hands respectfully joined.

Mangaraj then got up and went out to inspect his fields, wearing only a length of matha cloth, with an ocher-colored towel tied round his waist, and a big palm-leaf umbrella resting on his shoulder. Gobinda Puhan walked behind him talking about the management of the farm, while another farmhand, Pandia, followed carrying a pair of yokes. It was so early that some of the villagers were still in bed. Mangaraj and his farmhands came upon Pandit Sibu who, smelling snuff and with a tumbler of water in his left hand, was on his way to the fields to answer the call of nature. Suddenly discovering the master behind him, he hurriedly stepped aside. Putting the tumbler on the ground, he bent down, arching himself into the shape of a bow, joined his hands, and prayed aloud in ritual form for the zamindar's long life, fame, and prosperity. But Mangaraj took no notice of him and continued on. Once the zamindar was a safe distance away, the Brahmin slowly picked up the tumbler and recited a sloka:

Adya prātar evāniṣṭadarśhiniṃ jātaṃ, na jāne
kim anabhimataṃ darśayiṣyati.

The day begins with the sight of an evil man.
I know not what that day will bring!

Brahmins often chant slokas; there isn't much we can do about that.

Shyam Gochhaita was a Bauri, an untouchable. He had already planted his crop; his fields, on the outskirts of the village, were now as green as a parrot's wings. When Mangaraj and his party arrived, they found him busy working on an unfinished ridge. The zamindar went over to him and said tenderly, "Shyama, my dear son." Shyam was startled. He threw the spade down and flung himself at the zamindar's feet. "Get up, get up, oh, do get up dear son," said the master with a great show of affection. Shyam retreated some ten feet and stood with joined hands. There followed a long conversation between the zamindar and Shyam about all sorts of things. Dear reader, if we report everything that passed between the two, it will tire you out. Therefore, we will give you only the gist. The zamindar said that he took a fatherly interest in the welfare of Shyam's family. Shyam's father, Apartia, after all, used to come to him every evening to discuss problems related to farming, to seek advice on how to increase his yields, and so on. How unfortunate Shyam did not follow his example . . .

Suddenly the zamindar happened to glance at Shyam's plot of land. As if in shock, he exclaimed, in the tone of a concerned guardian, "Are you a fool, Shyama? What have you done? What kind of farmer are you? Why have you planted the seedlings so close together? There's no room for them to breathe. You must thin out at least half of them." Gobinda, too, took a good look at the field and heartily agreed. Shyam was trembling with fear. With his hands joined, he said, "Master, I plant my field like this every year. So does everyone else."

This irritated the master: "You fool, you won't even listen to good advice." He then turned to Gobinda, "Gobinda, dear boy, go and show him how it's done."

No sooner had these words been uttered than Gobinda and Pandia stripped the plot of half its seedlings, all this while Shyam kept howling and groveling at Mangaraj's feet. The zamindar became a bit angry, pointing out that whether or not he knew how to farm, Shyam must remember he had a loan to repay. Shyam stood petrified. At last the master relented and called out, "Gobinda, come away. Let him do whatever he pleases." Saying this, he proceeded toward his unplanted acre and a half, followed by his farmhands carrying two loads of seedlings.

CHAPTER FIVE

The Mangaraj Family

Ramachandra Mangaraj was responsible for a large household, which, apart from himself and his wife, included his three sons, their wives, the maidservants, and some twenty or more domestics—in all, around thirty mouths to feed. To tell the life story of each one would require going into far too much detail. And as you already know we are simply incapable of reporting irrelevant matters, telling lies, or exaggerating. Also, as the saying goes, unpleasant truths are better left unspoken; in other words, we are forced to forget half the truth and tell you only the other half.

The women in the house outnumbered the men and their voices drowned out all the others, except the barber's. The zamindar was always occupied with his own affairs. As for his sons, all three spent most of their time gambling, trapping gobara birds, brawling, and squabbling with the villagers; any time left over was devoted to smoking cannabis. The owner of the cannabis shop in the market once got angry with a customer and was

heard to remark, "Go away, I don't need your business. The zamindar's sons will keep me busy."

The zamindar and his sons rarely met. A village elder once
asked Mangaraj, "Why don't you spend more time with your
sons?" He replied quoting the Shastras:

Lālayet pañca varṣāṇi daśa varṣāṇi tāḍayet
Prāpte tu ṣoḍaśe varṣe putraṃ mitraṃ samācaret.

That is to say: a child dribbles helplessly until he is five; until he
reaches ten, he should be kept at a distance; and at sixteen, his father should mistreat him as he does his own friends.* In reality,
Mangaraj mistreated everyone: he would win their trust and
friendship and then drag them into the law courts to steal their
land. However, where his sons were concerned, the zamindar did
not strictly follow his own interpretation of the sloka. It is said he
was put off by them because they squandered his money on
liquor.

Mangaraj's wife slept alone in one corner of a room apart from
everyone else. Only when a wandering singer, a beggar, or someone poor, hungry, or thirsty arrived at her doorstep and asked for
her would she come out of her room. Propriety forbids us to
write about her daughters-in-law. What would people say if we
talked about these young women who were part of such a respectable family? What would be gained if we were to tell you
that they arose at one o'clock in the afternoon, that it was
evening by the time they finished their morning ablutions and
had their lunch, and that after that they took a short nap. When

---

*The lines are from the *Chanakyaniti* (by Chanakya, also known as Kantilya;
fourth to third century B.C.). The narrator deliberately mangles the translation.

they got up again night had fallen. Time before dinner was spent starting quarrels among the maidservants, and then settling them, and listening to village gossip. They did no work; peals of laughter could be heard until midnight.

Besides Rukuni, Marua, Chemi, Nakaphodi, Teri, Bimali, Suki, Pata, and Kausuli, there were many other maidservants in the house; we do not know all of them by name. Some were child widows, some had been widowed young, and some were born widows; only a few had husbands. Like birds of different feathers seeking shelter in a large tree, they had flocked to Mangaraj's house.* They kept arriving and leaving; it was impossible to keep track of their movements. When a crowd of maidservants with nothing to do gather in one place, what can they do but fight? Mangaraj's household was no exception to this eternal law. Until midnight it was filled with noise, like a fish market.

---

*These women were often indigent and helpless, and it is suggested later (see Marua's testimony in chapter 19) that Mangaraj exploited them.

CHAPTER SIX

Champa

Of the many people in Mangaraj's household, it was Champa, alias Mistress Champa, alias Harakala, whose relationship with the master was the most mysterious. Little too was known about her caste, her family background, or her lineage. And it was beyond anybody's power to decide whether she was the lady of the house or a mere maidservant. All that can be said is that Champa wielded a great deal of authority in Mangaraj's household, while his wife's presence was hardly felt there at all. Farmhands, laborers, the clerks in Mangaraj's office—everyone recognized Champa's power. Although one of her names was Harakala, the mistress of all wicked arts, no one dared address her as that. We should add that we have been unable to determine the origin of this name; we don't know whether it expresses praise or blame. One day, when someone told Champa that behind her back people called her this, she was outraged and burst into tears. She went straight to Mangaraj to complain. There was a hectic search for the culprit; people ran around for two days, but it was never discovered where the name had originated and how far it had spread. In the end, Mangaraj gave up, saying, "Don't worry, we'll find the person responsible. Beware, no one should call Champa Harakala!" That day, from one end of the village to the other, the villagers warned each other: "Beware, no one should call Champa Harakala!" For months, whenever they met, men and women, young and old, would repeat to one another: "Beware, no one should call Champa Harakala." Gradually the warning became more and more clipped: "Beware no one should call Champa"; then simply, "Beware." Finally, little children danced in the village street, clapping and singing:

"Beware, Beware!
Here comes Gabara Jena, Chowkidar!"

Children are always naughty, and so we shall take no notice of what they say. What is to be gained by paying attention to such things anyway?

At this point we should tell our readers that they will meet Champa often in the course of this tale, since she was very closely connected to Mangaraj's household. And so it is important for us to describe her person and her character carefully. The most revered and classical rules of literature require writers to draw the portrait of their heroes and heroines in traditionally pre-scribed ways. We are not in a position to violate these divinely sanctioned principles.

But our writers have a major weakness. When it comes to talk-ing about the heroine of their tales, they behave as though they have chanced upon something very delectable and do nothing but describe her beauty, forgetting everything else about her. As for us, it is not that we do not know how to describe the beauty of a heroine. Consider how ridiculously easy it is. According to classical literary techniques, all one has to do is find parallels between specific attributes of our heroine Champa and different fruits, such as bananas, jack-fruits, or mangoes, and common trees, leaves, and flowers. But such old-fashioned methods are no longer suitable; for our English-educated babus we now have to adopt an English style. Classical Indian poets compare the gait of a beautiful woman to that of an elephant. The babus frown on such a comparison; they would rather the heroine "galloped like a horse." The way English culture is rushing in like the first floods of the River Mahanadi, we suspect that our newly educated and civilized babus will soon appoint whip-cracking trainers to teach their gentle female companions to gallop.

In any case, we too are of the opinion that not a single classical poet has succeeded in finding a metaphor befitting the gait of a beautiful lady. How absurd to compare four-footed creatures, such as horses and elephants, to women! Our heroine, Champa, has only two legs; we must express our inability to imagine how she would look walking on all fours. As she has two legs, it might, however, not be inappropriate to liken her to a swan. Going strictly by the *Alankar Shastra*, apt similes and metaphors should be used at all times: a swan sometimes waddles; at other times, it half-jumps, half-flies. When our Champa made her way along the ridges of the rice fields, the ends of her Maniabandhi sari spreading like wings, she did indeed resemble a swan. As for her age, it is our guess that she was about thirty. However, we heard, from her very own lips, that she was a twenty-one-day-old baby when Mangaraj married. She must then have been much, much younger. To describe the beauty of such a youthful woman, one ought to exercise a great deal of caution and wisdom; one should be very liberal and broad-minded.

Of late, along with many other foreign goods, something called "ruchi"—taste—has been imported into our land. If you do not know what ruchi refers to, you are done for—people will consider you a fool, uncouth and uncivilized. This we learned the other day, when we saw what happened to the literary reputation of Upendra Bhanja, the great eighteenth-century Oriya poet. The poor fellow had managed to survive only because of the good karma his parents had accumulated. The way some of our modern critics and writers hounded him—only God knows how he escaped!* If such a great poet can be made to suffer like this, we see no hope for lesser mortals such as ourselves. So, with the blessings of our gurus and of the Brahmins, we have dared to compose a few lines according to modern ruchi. You may think us a pretender or an impostor, but here, in all humility, is a specimen:

Her breasts are bare, and her smile full of mischief.
She gallops like a mare, and like a cat's her eyes do glare,
Copper is the color of her hair; never does she shrink from
a brawl.
For a husband, she feels no need; she is at no man's beck
and call.
O beautiful woman!

---

*Upendra Bhanja, the eighteenth-century Oriya poet, wrote in the ornate tradition of classical Sanskrit poetry. The narrator refers to the way Senapati's modernist contemporaries attacked Bhanja's style (cf. the reference to the modernist literary journal *Bijuli* [literally "lightning"] a few lines later).

How graceful you look, dancing with a stranger.
O heavenly dancer!

Now, compare that with this couplet by Upendra Bhanja, written
in what nowadays would be described as bad ruchi:

Her thighs like the trunk of a banana plant
And her buttocks smoother than a plateau . . .

We dare not proceed any further. Perhaps Bijuli will flash again.
So now you know: we can compose poems in good taste, but we
dare not tell lies in broad daylight. We carried out a survey of the
physical attributes of several women, including Miss Chemi
Behera, in class five of Balipatna Girls School, and Miss S. M.
Ray—Miss Sasimukhi Ray—in a higher class of Bethune School.
None of these women have developed eyes like a cat's in deference to modern ruchi, or have cared to resemble heroines of
modern tasteful poems. So we will be considered crude and vul-
gar if we compose a truthful picture, but at the same time we cannot keep from telling the truth.

It is said the great Kalidasa once suffered from writer's block
while composing *Raghu Vamsa*. He overcame it by thinking about
his literary predecessors, which made it possible for him to write
again. So this is exactly what we shall do as well.* Kalidasa himself has left us a model based on which we can describe Champa's
charms. He wrote,

---

*A reference to the classical poet Kalidasa, who once had writer's block while
writing the story of the divine king Rama and overcame it by remembering his literary predecessors. The narrator's use of Kalidasa is humorous and parodic, since
his attitude to Champa is completely unlike Kalidasa's toward the god-king
Rama.

Tanvī śyāmā śikharidaśanā pakvabimbādharoṣṭhī.*

We interpret the line as follows: *tanu* means body, and since Champa has a body, she is *tanvi; shyama* refers to a complexion that is neither black nor white, therefore Champa's complexion can be called *shyama; shikhari* denotes a hill and *dashana* teeth: two of Champa's front teeth jut out, and so she perfectly answers to *shikhari dashana; pakva* means ripe and *bimba* is a red fruit; *adhorosthi* refers to the chin: Champa's lips and chin are reddened from endlessly chewing betel leaves; she can thus be called *pakva bimbadharosthi.*

Kalidasa goes on,

Madhye kṣāmā . . . stokanamrā . . .†

"Her breasts are so full and heavy that they touch each other, making the lady stoop a little . . ." Since we have not had the opportunity of seeing the parts of Champa's anatomy she keeps covered, we are absolutely unwilling to venture a description of them, even though old chap Kalidasa has himself provided us a model. We wholeheartedly subscribe to the precept "Seeing is believing."

Nevertheless, we are duty-bound to describe those parts we have actually seen. The following lines have been composed in the pajjhati metrical scheme.

Her eyes are decorated with kajal,
Her mouth full of betel,

*The literal translation of the line from Kalidasa is: "The color of her body is a shade dark, her teeth shapely and finely set, her lips are red like the bimba fruit." Senapati's narrator deliberately mistranslates and misinterprets the original Sanskrit, thus putting its authority (both in aesthetic and social matters) into question.

†The translation here is literal, though the tone is not quite right. The narrator's main point in the lines that follow is to ask, as in a court of law, how Kalidasa could possibly know the truth here since he could not have seen those parts of the woman's body.

Her body, massaged with oil and turmeric paste.
Draped in a sixteen-cubit sari,
She moves as fast as a she-dog.

Her hair has a top knot trimmed with flowers;
So heavy is she, one knows not
Whether she walks or runs.
Thick metal rings adorn her fingers.

Gesturing wildly she marches through the fields,
Her jingling anklets striking terror in the hearts of villagers.

And thus, dear reader, ends our literary account of Champa's beauty.

CHAPTER SEVEN

Goddess Budhi Mangala

O Goddess, in the form of a stone
You appear under a tree.
To you we always bow.
You, who ride clay elephants,
You, who bless barren women with children,
You, who cure dreaded diseases,
O Goddess Narayani, to you we bow.*

At the western edge of Asura Pond, to the right of the path that
runs between it and the village, there was a large, spreading
banyan tree. Its main trunk was hard to make out; a tangle of
twenty to twenty-five swollen prop roots covered half an acre of
land. Its foliage was so dense the sun could not break through. It

*The well-known Durga *vandana* (a paean to the goddess Durga) is here
slightly distorted and made colloquial (the goddess Budhi Mangala, after all,
unlike the universally recognized Durga, is only a local village deity). The distortion does not imply lack of devotion, however.

was an ancient tree. Village elders said that it had been the abode of Goddess Mangala since Satya Yuga, the Age of Truth. They had not seen any change in the tree since their childhood—it had grown neither larger nor smaller. Last year, on a moonless night, when a terrible storm blew down all the drumstick trees and banana plants in the village, not even a leaf from the banyan tree fell to the ground. Such is the power of the goddess!

Four of its prop roots were like veritable tree trunks, and among these was constructed the shrine of the village deity, Goddess Budhi (Old Lady) Mangala. There were two acres and a half of debottara land in her name: her shrine occupied roughly half an acre, and the rest provided for the upkeep of the priest and the goddess. The priest was very highly regarded in the village, particularly by the women. The goddess frequently appeared to him in his dreams and talked to him about everything. Everyone in the village brought the goddess the first fruits and vegetables from their gardens, such as bananas, brinjals, or pumpkins.

The goddess sat in the middle of a pucca platform. The statue was heavy and large; weighing not less than ten kilograms, it was bigger than the large stone slabs used to grind turmeric. The goddess's body was covered with a layer of vermilion two fingers thick. With her, there were four minor deities, and a little distance away, on the right-hand side of the platform, there was a pile of several small broken clay elephants and horses. If the goddess is offered clay elephants or horses she cures children from various kinds of ailments. Sometimes, even old people can be cured through such offerings. The goddess's stable was thus never short of such animals. However, she was not worshipped every day—ordinarily, she lay covered in leaves and dirt. Only when there was a wedding, when a child-wife attained puberty and went to join her husband, when somebody fell sick or someone wanted the deity to intercede for him or her, did worship at the goddess's shrine begin in earnest. When cholera broke out in the village, there was worship on a grand scale.

The goddess did not enjoy a regular monthly income, the way lowly clerks do. People gathered at her shrine only in times of danger and distress, as they do at the doors of doctors and lawyers. On such occasions her shrine sprang to life, and ceremonial pujas were financed by contributions from the villagers. The goddess was very powerful, and thanks to her protection the villagers came to no harm, although once in a while she would lose her temper and unleash her fury. But if the offerings were to her satisfaction, she would relent, and only a hundred villagers would die—the rest would be spared. Dear reader, you are an educated person. You might laugh and say, invoking modern science, "Why pray to the goddess at all? If you are sick, you should take medicine." For our part, although we cannot say how many, or which, barren ladies in the village the goddess has blessed with children, we nevertheless swear by the holy Nirmalya and declare that all women who now have children were most certainly barren before their marriages.

We have already referred to the path which ran past the goddess's shrine down to Asura Pond. It was used mostly by the village women. Every day, along this path, came a woman in her thirties, carrying a pitcher of water. She would stop before the goddess, make obeisance, sweep and wash the place of worship, and water the tree. Every evening, she would light a lamp there and murmur a prayer. The villagers had seen her do this for the last six months. No one knew her thoughts or what she prayed for; she was very shy and kept her face modestly covered with the end of her sari. She never mixed with anyone, she talked to no one.

Every afternoon the young cowherds of the village played near the goddess's seat, leaving their cows to graze in the fields. One afternoon, they suddenly stopped; clutching their staves, and stood huddled around the goddess. Ten to fifteen villagers joined them out of curiosity. Why were there offerings to the goddess when there had been no puja? She wore a fresh layer of turmeric paste and scattered around her were hibiscus flowers, garlands of satbarga flowers, and khai and ukhuda as food offerings.

The goddess's ceremonial puja, her ritual worship, was always a major event in the village. Contributions were raised, drums were beaten, and all the villagers assembled in the evening for that purpose. Private prayers were offered in the same manner. But no one had heard the drums yesterday, nor had there been puja in the evening. Where then did all these offerings come from? One of the cowherds suddenly cried out, "What's this, what's this?" Everyone rushed towards him and saw a large hole some three arm-lengths from the platform on which the goddess sat. It was large enough to hold a man.

In no time, the news spread throughout the village, and everyone came running. Mangaraj, too, lost no time getting there. After much discussion it was decided that the goddess had appeared in the dead of the previous night to help a devotee in distress, and that the hole was made by the tiger she rode. Mangaraj proclaimed, "The tiger still seems to be there, inside the hole." This made the villagers flee. Mangaraj then glanced meaningfully at Rama, and walked away. Our guess is that this was some kind of signal. The hole disappeared the same day.

For several days, the villagers could not stop talking about these events. Bhima's mother, the barber-woman, said, "I am now one hundred and twenty, or maybe even one hundred and thirty years old. I attended the wedding ceremonies of all these old men you see in the village, when they were young. Compared to me, they are only children. I have seen the goddess four times, including this one. Yesterday, at midnight, I went out to relieve myself. Suddenly there was the smell of incense, and I heard the tinkle of anklets. Looking up, I saw the goddess riding her tiger. What a huge one it was! I have seen many in my day, but this was the biggest. It was seven to eight arm lengths long; its head was black like a buffalo's. It glared at me and I fled for my life, banging the door shut behind me."

Four to five old men in the village supported her story and said they too had heard the tiger. Rama, the weaver, claimed that that morning he had noticed the pugmarks. It was now established, beyond a doubt, that the goddess had appeared in the village the night before.

CHAPTER EIGHT

Zamindar Sheikh Dildar Mian

Sheikh Keramat Ali used to live in Ara district, and had now moved to Midnapore. Everyone called him Ali Mian, or Mian for short; we will do the same. Ali Mian began his career as a horse trader. He would purchase horses at the West Harihar Chhatar fair and sell them in Bengal and Orissa. Once he sold a horse to the district magistrate of Midnapore. The Sahib was very pleased with it and condescended to inquire about Mian's business and income. When Mian told him there was not much profit in horse trading, the Sahib, wanting to offer him a job, asked if he knew how to read and write. Mian replied, "Huzoor, I know Persian. If you would kindly give me pen and paper, I could show you I can write my full name."

In the past, the Persian language had been held in high favor; it was the language of the court. With a sharp and pitiless pen, God has inscribed a strange fate for India: yesterday, the language of the court was Persian, today it is English. Only He knows which language will follow tomorrow. Whichever it may be, we know for certain that Sanskrit lies crushed beneath a rock for ever. English pundits say, "Sanskrit is a dead language." We would go even further: "Sanskrit is a language of the half-dead."

Anyhow, our Mian got a job through the Sahib's mercy; he was now a thana daroga. He survived in this job for thirty years without much trouble, and during that time amassed considerable property. He acquired four zamindaris and built himself a big house; he owned farms and gardens and a large number of household goods. In those days, the zamindaris of Orissa were auctioned off in Calcutta. One time, while visiting that city in connection with a murder case, Mian Sahib made a bid for the zamindari of Fatepur Sarsandha, and was successful. You may find this puzzling—how could a thana daroga, who was only an inspector in the Bengal police, raise enough money to buy a zamindari? Nevertheless, the details herein presented are accurate and precise; you may read on with your eyes closed.

We will now recount a well-known incident. Once a deputy collector decreed in his court in favor of a Brahmin called Gobinda Panda. The Brahmin, overjoyed, blessed him, "O Deputy babu, may you become a police inspector."* We believe you have gotten the point; for intelligent people hints usually suffice. Take another example: Moti Sila is now one of the richest businessmen in Calcutta. He began by selling empty bottles. A country liquor merchant once lamented, "Look at how strange are the ways of the world! Moti Sila became a man of crores by selling empty bottles; I sell full ones, and I'm a beggar." We fear

---

*The Brahmin, ignorant of the hierarchies of the bureaucracy, assumes that the "inspector" is more powerful than a "deputy collector." In the corrupt world of colonial society, with its many petty authorities, an unscrupulous police officer could make a great deal of money.

that some babus with B.A. and M.A. degrees might say, together with this merchant, "Alas, Ali Mian, who could not even hold a pen properly, became a zamindar just by writing his name. Even though we can write long essays and hold a pen correctly, we starve." Dear babus, don't you know that it is one's fate which ultimately prevails, not one's wisdom or character.

Ali Mian had only one son, Sheikh Dildar Mian, alias Chhota Mian. The daroga took every care to ensure his son would become a properly qualified and accomplished man. To teach him Persian, he engaged a private tutor for many years, and by the time Chhota Mian was fifteen, he had already mastered the alphabet and elementary spelling. Now he was twenty-two; what would people say if they saw him still sitting, bent over his books, in front of a tutor? Besides, it was unbearable to keep his friends waiting, while having to do his lessons. Even more painful was the tutor's claim that alcohol turned men into beasts. That was the last straw.

One afternoon the tutor was enjoying a nap after his midday meal. His white flowing beard covered his neck and chest like the straw bundles local fishermen lay out when they weave their nets. Suddenly a live ember fell on his beard and soon burned into his chest. He scrambled out of bed shouting, "Horror, horror," and tried to put out the fire. The ember broke into pieces and sparks fell on his clothes. The burning beard now glowed like a sparkler, and the tutor jumped about the room, shouting and trying to blow out the fire. The great sage Valmiki has not left us an adequate description of how the monkey god Hanuman's face looked when it caught fire as he was setting the kingdom of Lanka aflame. Therefore it would be improper for us to even contemplate comparing the face of Chhota Mian's tutor with that of

Hanuman. The Shastras say: "When wise men face the danger of losing everything, they choose to part with half." Acting perhaps on this, the tutor sacrificed half his beard, and thanking Allah, saved the rest. He bolted the door of his room, stayed inside all night, and no one ever saw him in Midnapore again.

When Ali Mian learned of this, he remarked, "No matter; my Dilu has already gained all the knowledge he needs. I have acquired all my wealth and property simply by being able to write my name. As for Dilu, he is so much more learned than that: the other day I set him a test, and he reeled off not only his own name, but words such as Calcutta, Midnapore, elephant, horse, farm, garden, and so on. The district magistrate will surely make him a daroga if he finds out how much he has learned. But I have kept his talents a secret because I will not let my Dilu work as a mere servant of the government. He is but a child; he could not take the strain."

Later Ali Mian called in his son, sat him down, and gave him much advice on the management of his property. Mian cautioned his son to be particularly alert as regards the zamindari in Orissa: "Be careful son, the Mohantys of Orissa are thieves. It is only because I pay close attention to my accounts that they have not been able to outwit me. Let me give you an example of how they cheat: one, two, three, four—that's how everyone counts. But do you know how the Mohantys count? One times one is one, two times two is four. See, they mention one, two and four; but where did three go? It's the three rupees the Mohantys steal."

But all this is about the past. We were forced to retell it in order to introduce the present zamindar. The previous one, Sheikh Keramat Ali, had been dead for five years and Chhota Mian, alias Sheikh Dildar, had succeeded him.

It was evening. Sheikh Dildar sat in his office, a large pucca room in a big and spacious house. A big carpet covered the floor of the office; it was very old and tattered, stained in places with blotches of oil, burned here and there by embers from hookahs, its edges frayed. On the carpet near the wall lay a mattress with a Benarasi bedspread covering it, and pressed against the wall was a huge Benarasi pillow, with two small pumpkin-shaped pillows on either side. Sheikh Dildar was seated on the bedspread. He wore a loose silk pajama suit, embroidered with jari, and a satin chapkan, a Benarasi cap on his head. In each of his ears he had a wad of perfumed cotton. In front of him stood slender vases containing attar and rose water. Usually he smoked a seven-cubit-long pipe from an ornate hookah, which he kept spluttering nearby. On top of the hookah smoldered a live ember, duly covered. Four silver strings dangled from the tray holding the ember. Today, however, the pipe of the hookah lay at his feet like a sick supplicant prostrating himself before Lord Mahadeva. The fortunes of human beings turn like a wheel; so too does the fortune of inanimate objects. A worn-out broom, tumblers with beaks, a few small hookahs, twists of tobacco, cannabis ash, onion peel, goat droppings—many useful, as well as discarded, objects like these lay scattered about the room. The old carpet was smeared with betel juice. We can safely infer, drawing on our innate perspicuity, that somebody cleaned this room from time to time; how else would so much rubbish accumulate in the corners? There were cracks in the ceiling, and here and there, spiders in their webs waited keenly for insects, like lawyers in their offices lined with books in glass cases. Sparrows cheerfully twittered and played on the crossbeams of the ceiling, occasionally dropping twigs and bits of straw.

But the space beneath them was silent and cheerless. Mian sat gloomily, his hand on his cheek. Even Napoleon did not sit so despondently after his defeat at Waterloo, with the British looking to send him to St. Helena; no, he could not afford to brood like Mian. Seated in front of Mian were seven companions, all dozing, or perhaps deep in thought. Ustad Bakaul Kahn sat hugging his knees, which propped up his bearded chin. In one corner of the room a tanpura lay helpless like a divorced Muslim woman, and the tablas rolled beside it like ritually impure earthen vessels in the fields. In another corner, a servant named Fatua used his right thumb to knead some stuff in his left palm, and from time to time his middle finger soaked it with drops of water. The munshi, Zaheer Bux, holding a piece of paper, stood in front of the zamindar as if he were a thief brought before a deputy collector. Mian Sahib, his eyes closed, heaved a deep sigh, and said, "What is the way out now?"

The munshi answered, "Oh, your highness, I have been running around all day long, but I have failed everywhere. Ramdas, the moneylender, said to me, 'I have already loaned out twenty thousand rupees against the mortgage and four thousand without collateral. I can't lend any more.' And we owe the shopkeepers in the local market four thousand rupees. Yesterday they refused to give anything on credit."

Mian burst out, "You incompetent idiot, you luckless wretch. I asked you to manage my estate because I thought you were my friend and an able man. For you, I threw out Ram Sarkar, who had worked twenty long years for my father. You are so useless . . ."

Zaheer Bux replied, "Huzoor, how can you call me incompetent? In the past five years I have arranged twenty-five thousand rupees on credit. Ram Sarkar could not get you a loan of a single rupee."

Mian said, "All right, let that be. Now think of my izzat, my honor and dignity. I can lose my wealth, but I cannot bear the loss of my izzat, for once it's lost, it's gone forever."

His companions, who were dozing, suddenly spoke out in one voice, "How true, how true!"

"Go mortgage whatever you like," Mian ordered his munshi, "household goods or even the zamindari, but make sure you get the money for the party tonight. It's already late, do something fast. We don't need a lot. One hundred rupees for the nautch girl, and another hundred for a pulau for her companions and my friends should be enough."

His friends agreed, "You are absolutely right. What would we do with more than that?"

Hanumian, a friend of the zamindar, submitted, "Huzoor, this nautch girl Khatum-unnisa is highly gifted. She's a first-class dancer from Kashmir. In her command of the ragas and her skill as a dancer, she's perfection incarnate. Normally she would consider it beneath her to come to this part of the country. But because she's traveling and it falls on her way, she happens to be here; she has turned down invitations from the Nawabs of Murshidabad and Lucknow, and from several Badshahs. It's only your power and high repute that have made her agree to come."

All present concurred in chorus, "Our Huzoor is known everywhere. Can anyone who has ever tasted a pulau offered by him forget its divine taste?"

At this moment the attendant, Sheikh Fazu, came in, saluted and informed the zamindar, "Huzoor, a moneylender from your zamindari in Orissa has come to pay his respects."

He was ordered to bring the moneylender in. The visitor entered the room, placed five rupees at the zamindar's feet as a token of respect and saluted him three times. Then he saluted everyone present, including the servant. At this, Mian remarked, "He seems a good judge of men."

All agreed with Mian and shouted, "Yes, he's a good judge of men, a good judge of men." Mian then turned to the visitor and asked him his name.

"Ramachandra Mangaraj," replied the visitor.

"Ramachandra Mamlabaj?" asked Mian.

"No, Huzoor, it's Mangaraj."

"All right, Rama Chander Mangaraj."

Mangaraj announced, "My Lord, I have brought you a few small gifts. If you permit, I shall place them before you."

"Very good. Bring them in."

The list of gifts, inscribed on a palm leaf, was then read out: five baskets of fine-grained rice; one bharana and eight nautis of mung dal, and thirty-two nautis of toor dal, in two baskets; twenty-five seers of ghee, in an earthen vessel; five hands of green cooking bananas; two hands of ripe bananas; and eight bisas of potatoes.

Mian commented, "Very fine rice. Very fine rice. It'll be good for our pulau, and the ghee is also excellent."

Mangaraj said, "Huzoor, you are the lord of the world. For fifteen generations we have survived on your charity. What I have brought today is nothing. If you would be so kind as to so direct me, I will always supply ghee, dal, and rice for the pulau."

"Miaow, Mian-ow Mi-an-ow," sang out the tanpura, when the ustad struck its strings in joyous expectation.

"Boom, boom, boom, tak-dhina-dhin," answered the tabla.

Mian issued orders, "Make arrangements to start the cooking."

Christians believe that when the angels of heaven blow the trumpet on the day of judgment, the dead will rise from their graves. Until now the party lay dead; it was resurrected at the sound of Mangaraj's tinkling coins. Mian put his mouth to the hookah, took a few hearty puffs, and expelled clouds of smoke, which enveloped him like mist surrounding a black mountain. Just as the government digs canals to distribute water from the Mahanadi to various districts, Mian flooded the faces in the room with smoke from his pipe.

"Mein, Mein," bleated the billy goat dragged before Mian. The animal, meant for the pulau, was priced at two-and-a-half rupees. Mangaraj, startled, exclaimed, "What! Two-and-a-half rupees? My God, how can that be?"

"How much would it cost in your village?" asked Mian.

Like a doctor examining a patient, Mangaraj felt every part of the animal and replied, "Well, not a lot. Just four or six paise. If Huzoor so wishes, I can send forty or sixty like this for a pulau any day. May I humbly submit that Huzoor has not employed the right sort of servant to manage his zamindari. That's why there's so much waste. How could a goat cost two-and-a-half rupees?"

On hearing this, Mian and his friends were overwhelmed with joy; indeed, their feelings cannot be described in words. The Board of Directors of the East India Company in England could not have felt as elated when they heard of Clive's victory at Plassey, because at that time the directors still lived in awe of the Delhi Durbar. The court musician's voice rang out, swelling through the notes of the raga *Puriya*. All were mad with joy; peals of laughter filled the room. Only Mangaraj sat anxiously in a corner, with joined hands, like a trapper watching birds peck at grain strewn under a net. We know very well how Mangaraj's mind was working. At that very moment he was perhaps thinking, "Come, sweet birdies, step into my trap."

A servant rushed in and announced that the nautch girl had arrived. "Oh, God, we had forgotten all about her." The ustad was a responsible person, and he immediately reminded the party that a hundred rupees had to be offered to her as a token of welcome. Worries about how this amount could be arranged began agitating Mian and his friends. Even the British Parliament does not become this agitated when it finalizes the budget for India. No one could suggest a way out, and there was no time for discussion. Mangaraj decided that this was the right moment, and spoke up, "Huzoor, when such a humble servant is at your service, why need you worry?"

Once more, fulsome praise and greetings from all sides were showered on him. Mian announced, "Well done, Mangaraj, you shall definitely be rewarded for the good work you have done today. Moreover, you will be given four annas interest on every rupee you have given us."

Mangaraj hastened to add, "Oh, Ram, oh, Ram! Huzoor, I have no interest in such a thing."

The ustad thought, "What, he does not take interest? He must be a very honest man. The Holy Quran lists taking interest among the twenty-five forbidden deeds."

Historians say it took Clive less time to get the Bengal Subedari from the emperor of Delhi than it takes one to buy and sell a donkey. How long do you think it will take Mangaraj to get the zamindari of Fatepur Sarsandha from Mian?

CHAPTER NINE

Village News

Fatepur Sarsandha was a huge zamindari, assessed at 5,208 rupees and 6 annas per year. It comprised five villages: Ramanagar, Balia, Handi Khai, Sautunia, and Gobindapur. Of these, the largest was Gobindapur, with five hundred families from different castes. There was one shop in the village; it sold dal, rice, tobacco, salt, oil, and anything else the villagers needed. You could, in a pinch, even buy two or three paise worth of ghee. The shopkeeper also stocked three-generations-old dasamula, a common ayurvedic medicine, and vaidyas—country doctors—from villages far and near ordered it from him.

The village had an elongated shape: two rows of houses stood on either side of a long winding path on the north and the west banks of Asura Pond. Although there was a fairly wide section toward the middle, for the most part the path was not more than ten to twelve arm-lengths wide. Every house had its own approach from the main path, and heaps of compost stood in front of each one. There were a few empty lots, where, every morning, cattle were kept tethered, and here and there along the village path a few bullock carts could be found. The village was divided into three quarters: the Saanta or master's quarter, the weavers' quarter, and the Brahmin quarter.

In the Saanta quarter was to be found the residence of Ramachandra Mangaraj himself. This was a very busy place, for Mangaraj's kacheri was open late into the night. The village shop was also here. The other quarters of the village usually became quiet soon after sunset.

The Brahmin quarter was called by its traditional name, a sasana. Here, five hundred Brahmins from seventy-two families lived. There were 150 coconut trees on either side of the path through this quarter, and, under one of them, there was a large stone pedestal. It was the seat of Lord Baladeba. Ten or fifteen arm-lengths away stood some young coconut trees. The space around these had been cleared for the Brahmins to meet and discuss such grave matters as snuff, bhang, rites and rituals, income from clients, and so on. On occasion, bitter squabbles broke out; it can be assumed that the Brahmins were quarreling over sharing gifts of grain from their clients. On hearing the racket, people would remark that the Brahmins were fighting like dogs over a handful of rice. We, for our part, disapprove of such remarks, for they are made by people who are quite ignorant and who forget that Brahmins, even if they are utterly worthless, are the kings of all thirty-six castes. It is absolutely incorrect to compare them to dogs. The comparison is quite inappropriate: Brahmins fight over rice offered to departed souls, whereas dogs fight over rice left over by the living; rice offered to departed souls is merely soaked, whereas that left over by the living is cooked; dogs bite each other, whereas Brahmins beat each other—they do not bite or scratch. When vultures are seen overhead you know there is a corpse lying somewhere. Likewise, when Brahmins are seen marching in groups, their sacred threads shining across their chests, people know that someone has died.

The Brahmins once owned five hundred acres of land, which they had obtained through a copper-plate deed from the Marhatta Subedar on the condition that they bless him three times a day. But we know that collecting the cattle from the grazing fields, smoking out insects from the cowsheds, serving rice gruel to the farmhands, and so on, kept the Brahmins busy all day long. When could they find time to bless their benefactor? One day Bhabani Bahinipati, a Brahmin, complained, "How can we bless anyone when all our land is gone?" What he said was not entirely untrue. Over the last ten years, four hundred of the five hundred acres of Brahmin land had been sold off. The remaining few acres were safe because Mangaraj took care of them. He was well known for his concern for cows, which are held sacred, and for Brahmins. He would not allow a stray cow to wander uncared for; he would take her home and make her his own. We noticed that the lowly panas regularly collected such cows for Mangaraj, in return for small rewards. Not counting the bullocks, there were now more than three hundred cows in Mangaraj's shed. He took the trouble of looking after that many, because he could not bear to see the sacred animals wandering helplessly about the village. However, when the burden became too great, he would sell off some of them to Muslim cattle merchants. Mangaraj bought the land from the Brahmins and looked after it with the same concern he showed for the cows. What could the Brahmins do but sell off their land? For one thing, Brahmins know nothing about cultivating land. Secondly, thieves habitually stole the harvest only from land belonging to the Brahmins. Now that a portion of the Brahmins' land had passed into Mangaraj's hands, the thieves were reluctant to enter the rice fields. Some say the land was acquired very cheaply, that Mangaraj purchased it for five rupees an acre. Such people misunderstand the situation. Aren't five bharanas of grain harvested from one bharana of seed? Should Mangaraj's rupees lie barren, should they yield nothing?

Pandit Sibu's house stood in the middle of the Brahmin quarter. He used to say that his grandfather, Biki Khadanga, could recite the entire text of the Satapada Grammar effortlessly, any time he was asked. He had not neglected to master the Naisadhanta also. Conjugations and declensions in Sanskrit came as naturally to him as song to a cuckoo. All his texts were carefully kept in a wooden chest in the puja room. Pandit Sibu performed his puja daily. Like his grandfather, he too, was a great scholar. He could recite all five chapters of the Amarkosha dictionary, without ever looking at the text. The pandit's stepfather's uncle's son's brother's brother-in-law's cousin had studied the *Nyaya Shastra* at Nabadwip. To sum up, it was because of the Khadanga family that scholarship had not altogether disappeared from the Brahmin quarter. Twice a day, the Brahmin children came and did their lessons on the pandit's front verandah. Here, they were taught about forty-one rituals and different methods of counting. A few of them even went on to receive higher education, up to first or second standard in primary school.

On the western side of the village, in the weavers' quarter, lived 150 families. The village path running through this quarter looked neat and clean; there were no compost pits or manure heaps anywhere. You might suppose that a regulation was in force here, and that the municipal carts came daily to take away the rubbish. We warn you not to jump to conclusions before hearing us out; we are writing on the basis of a thorough investigation and of ample proof. We would not want you to get any wrong ideas, for then there would be no point in our working so painstakingly hard. Also, it would be against our nature to record irrelevant things. We refuse to pay attention to anything that has not been supported by irrefutable proof or that is not consistent with the principles of logic as they are laid down in the *Nyaya Shastra*. We are prepared to logically establish everything we write, so that you will have no legitimate complaints. Now, consider what the *Nyaya Shastra* says about good logical reasoning.* Why is there smoke on the mountain? Because there is fire inside. Why is the Mahanadi River in spate? Because it rained at its source. This is the eternal relation between and action or event and its cause. No action exists without a cause: flooding exists because of its cause, rain. Likewise, we could prove, with unassailable arguments, that there is an immutable relation between cow dung and cows. You would definitely agree that if there is no cause, there is no effect. Therefore, from the absence of cow dung in the weavers' quarters, you can infer that there were no cows there. In other words, since there were no cows, there was no cow dung. Yet a doubt may still trouble you. Cows are not jungle beasts like tigers or bears; they are domestic animals, and it is natural that they should live in a village, and not in the jungle. Just as wherever there is water, there are fish, wherever there is a village, there are domestic animals. You know the weavers' quarter is a village; so then, why are there no domestic animals in

---

*A self-serving reference to the kind of syllogistic reasoning discussed in the *Nyaya Shastra*; the example of smoke and mountain is from the *Nyaya* tradition.

it? There are many defects in the design of God's creation: either God was incompetent, or else He was careless. You know that animals, birds, insects, and fleas have to be either male or female; yet there is sometimes a neuter among them. Similarly, even though the weavers' quarter was in a village, it had no domestic animals. In other words, pursuing the previously mentioned metaphor concerning animals, birds, and insects, this village might be described as a neuter: it had neither wild animals such as tigers and bears, nor domestic animals such as cows. There must be some reason for this. There is a reason for everything. Whenever grammarians have trouble defining something, they get round the difficulty by declaring that something is an exception! However, we regard this as cheating. Such is not our way. Never mind. Allow us to explain why there were no cows in the weavers' quarter. It is written in the Bible that one cannot serve two masters at the same time. Holy scribes everywhere speak in a cryptic manner, which is why we need interpreters to help us make sense of the original texts. Had there not been interpreters such as Mallinatha, Mathuranath, and Sridhar, texts like the *Raghuvansa*, the *Nyaya*, and the *Bhagavata* would have gone unopened and unread. Unless the saying is interpreted, it will be difficult for us to understand. We recognize that you are able to read the Bible by yourself, but then not everyone is as competent as you. Let us now offer an interpretation of the biblical saying quoted above. Another way of expressing it would be to say that a man cannot do two things at once; for example, since a weaver spends the entire day weaving, when would he find time for farming? Why would you need bullocks when you do not till the land? And, if there are no bullocks, how can there be cow dung?

Obviously, since there was no cow dung in the weavers' quarters, the village path remained clean.

Today, in the nineteenth century, the sciences enjoy great prestige, for they form the basis of all progress. See, the British are white-skinned, whereas Oriyas are dark in complexion. This is because the former have studied the sciences, whereas the latter have no knowledge of these. We, for our part, have just begun to take an interest in the new culture, and with its help we are able to explain many things. Just pay attention to what we say, and you will see how exact the sciences are. Let us now consider one scientific law: two objects cannot occupy the same space. You might say that one bowl can contain milk, as well as water. But, let us explain this law in greater detail. What is meant is that two objects cannot occupy the same space at the same time. When the bowl is full of milk, how can it also hold water? Now, the weaver has to use the space inside his house as well as outside for weaving. Clothes are woven indoors, thread is spun outdoors. Therefore, in accordance with the above scientific law, it would be impossible for cow dung to be outside, where, before clothes are woven inside, cotton thread is stretched, treated, and cleaned. Now, men and women worked together to weave clothes: the women busily soaked the thread in rice gruel and wound it around the spindles. When would they find time to take the cows out to graze and bring them back, and so on? There were many other reasons why weavers did not keep cows, but we will not go into them here. We cannot tolerate digressions from our original subject.

CHAPTER TEN

Bhagia, the Weaver, and Saria, His Wife

At the edge of the weavers' quarter is the Bhagavataghara and the temple to Lord Dadhi Bamana, built from cash contributions raised among the weavers. Do you know how cash contributions are raised? Although you may need no explanation, the new babus do, for they are educated: they have studied and have mastered profundities. Ask a new babu his grandfather's father's name and he will hem and haw, but the names of the ancestors of England's Charles the Third will readily roll off his tongue. To be considered a scholar, it is necessary to have read about the English or the French; there is no point in learning about oneself or one's neighbor. But all this is probably not very important. We should not run the risk of displeasing our babus with such unnecessary remarks.

This is how cash contributions were raised: if a weaver did something wrong, the five elders of the community imposed a fine; the money from the fine was called a cash contribution.

However, if a weaver could not afford the fine, the elders might relent and pay it themselves. Cash contributions were administered by the headman of the community, called the paramanika. The Dadhi Bamana temple was built from such contributions. The rule concerning cash contributions was enforced in all trading communities throughout our country. Alas, this fine custom is gradually disappearing. Today, the law courts have opened wide their doors, and people have become educated and civilized. Why should anyone heed the rule of the five elders anymore? English law warns, "Watch out my friend. If we obtain legally conclusive proof that you have committed a crime, you shall be punished." A clever man answers, "Sir, I know how to make sure you don't get any proof." "No worry, no worry," adds the lawyer, patting him on the back. "Just bring me cash. I can make black, white and white, black." Under this system, the clever and the rich get off, even though, in truth, they are guilty of hundreds of crimes; while the simple and the poor get into trouble and are harassed for their innocence in the law courts. The expense incurred in court cases today makes beggars of both parties, since all sorts of worthless people thrive off their misfortune. But in the old system, it was impossible to deceive the five elders. Moreover, the fine imposed on the real culprit was spent on a good cause.

It is commonly believed that there exists a relation between stupidity and weavers. If someone does something stupid, people immediately exclaim, "Hey, are you a weaver or what?" In other words, the person is considered stupid, "as stupid as a weaver." If you are a civilized babu, you will surely believe that this saying is absolutely true, because you know how the Dadhi Bamana temple was built. You are probably wondering why the community's cash contributions were misused in such a manner. Surely, the money could have been used, instead, to establish a scholarship in the name of the collector Sahib, or to name a hospital after the governor-general. Why, of all things, a temple?

It is, of course, our duty to say only those things that will please you. However, what you have just suggested seems to us somewhat odd. We are not saying that you are wrong, but let us explain about weaver intelligence. "Weaver intelligence" is a complicated expression. You know that a lotus is called pankaja because grows in panka; it does not follow from this, however, that all that grows in mud—weeds, slime, shellfish, snails— should be called a lotus. Similarly, the word *weaver* denotes a stupid person, but not every stupid person is a weaver. Think of the Manchester weavers, who made the British Parliament tremble. It is thanks to them that you can present yourself as a babu. To call into question the intelligence of those very weavers amounts to an act of ingratitude. If you probe deeper into the matter you will find that all our ancestors were weavers. You won't have to study archeology to prove this; the presence of collectively funded and built temples in every village is proof enough.

It is our belief that to come to a conclusion without having considered both sides of a matter is typical of weaver thinking. Let us try to find out if the temples were indeed built using weaver funds. These incorrigible rustics, as you probably know, work all day making a living, and in the evening, eat a few handfuls of rice and go to sleep. There are no missionaries in the village, nor are there any libraries. Where, then, could they receive religious instruction? Every day, the conch is blown in the morning and in the evening, and the bell is rung in the temple. This announces to everyone—from children to old men—that a divine presence is guiding the universe. In the temple, there is a

Bhagavatagadi, where the sacred books are kept. On festive occasions such as Radhastami, Janmastami, and during the month of Kartika, the villagers gather to listen to the sacred books, which are read collectively. If there were no temple, there would be no religious practice of this sort, no chance to listen to God's name or to the scriptures. Whenever a stranger arrives in the village, or if a villager is unable to cook at home, for whatever reason, he can pay two paise to the temple cook and get a bellyful of prasad. Also, it is within the confines of the temple that the five elders meet to settle disputes or sit in judgment over the wrongdoings of the villagers. It might be easier for you to understand the value of a temple if we use English instead of native terms: the temple in the village functioned as a church, a public library, a restaurant, and a town hall. And let us leave it at that; we need to move on to other important matters.

Like all trading communities, the weavers too had a headman called the paramanika, without consulting whom no caste rites could be performed. It was the paramanika who distributed areca nuts to the community when there was a marriage or when a bride left her parents' home for her in-laws' on reaching puberty. In return, the paramanika received a dhoti and an areca nut. If a villager brought a complaint, the paramanika would send five areca nuts to the five elders, inviting them to convene. At community gatherings, flowers and sandal paste were offered to the paramanika first, and at feasts, people would only begin eating after he had blessed the food pronouncing the name of Lord Krishna. The title "Paramanika" was hereditary: only the son of a paramanika or a member of his family could become a paramanika; not just anyone from the village could assume the title.

The present paramanika was Bhagia Chandra. Poor Bhagia

was a simple man: his mind had not yet been tainted by lies and deceit; he accepted, on good faith, whatever he was told. People described him as a stupid weaver. Dear reader, we can easily read your thoughts; we can figure them out through hints and guesses. Your face reveals everything, everything you want to say or are going to say, everything you are thinking now or might think in the future. You are thinking, "These weavers are all stupid. Simply because his father was the paramanika, these weavers have made stupid Bhagia their headman and are paying their respects to him. Stupid weavers, if you wanted a headman, you should have elected a wise and competent one, just as people elect a member of Parliament or the president of the United States. Instead, you have made a simpleton your headman just because his father used to be your paramanika." Dear reader, what you have just formulated is absolutely true and we cannot respond. Your argument is so convincing, it leaves no room for disagreement. We have been taking the weavers' side all along; now, we must change our mind. We vow that henceforth we will stay away from weavers. Nevertheless, esteemed readers, we plead ignorance of the world. We wish to learn more about weavers. Oh, knowledgeable reader, kindly enlighten us.

If you are a Hindu, you will, of course, honor the Vedas, the Vedantas, and other Hindu Shastras. According to the Shastras,

Śamo damas tapaḥ śaucaṃ santoṣaṃ kṣāntir ārjavaṃ
madbhaktiś ca dayā satyaṃ brahmaprakṛtaysas tv imāḥ.

Self-control, meditation, performance of duties, purity, contentment,
forgiveness, honesty, simplicity: these are the hallmarks of
Brahminhood.

A Brahmin having these qualities is worthy of devotion, worship, and respect. We are willing to smear our foreheads a hundred times with dust from the feet of such a one. But now, let us describe a modern Brahmin:

Listen to me, O king Pariksha.
These are the qualities of Sundar Tripathy,
A Brahmin of our time:
He takes rice gruel with salted fish,
Of learning he knows nothing;
Adorned with the sacred thread and sandal paste,
He pulls weeds from the rice fields;
A meal of curd and rice flakes, he always craves,
Prayers and the Gayatri Mantra, he never chants;
He catches small fish in the rice fields,
And never opens his sacred books;
He steals rice from clients who are his hosts,
At learned gatherings, he never says a word.*

You bow low before Sundar Tripathy because he was lawfully begotten by a Brahmin. He is your family priest, because his father was your family priest. Of course, we do not dare tell you such things to your face, so we have written them here. It is also written in the Shastras,

Ajñānatimirāndhasya jñānāñjanaśalākayā
Cakṣur unmīlitaṃ yena tasmai śrigurave namaḥ

*In the Oriya original, this is composed in the traditional verse form of the sixteenth-century Oriya *Bhagavata*, which would have been familiar to all of Senapati's readers.

He who applies the balm of knowledge
And opens our eyes blinded by the disease of ignorance,
*To a guru like him, we bow.**

Now tell us, is a person your guru because he is learned or because he is the son of a guru? It is better to forget these things; what will we gain from them, after all? At any rate, by now, we had hoped to be able to tell you more about weavers. We ought not to be finding fault with babus; we are like the proverbial pot calling the kettle black. Probing deeply into these matters would be as futile as swimming through mist. Like village women chattering while pounding rice, we have dragged dignified persons like you into our silly story. Whenever a matter comes up for discussion, everyone present puts in a word or two, no matter if what they say is relevant or not. At a sankirtan, even a dumb person opens his mouth wide, as if he is singing!

Let us now return to the village. Like a vessel with a well-fitting lid, our poor Bhagia, the simple-minded weaver, had a wife who was no more intelligent than he. Her name was Saria. She was about twenty-five years old. Now that you know what a simpleton she was, is there any need for us to describe her other virtues? You see, it is not good to rely on the opinion of others. You must try to use your wits to draw your own conclusions. Do not depend entirely on us. Once you grasp the main technique of getting at a matter through inference, everything will be clear to you. When you hear that a young woman is a princess, you naturally infer that she is extremely beautiful, virtuous, incomparable, the equal of the goddesses Lakshmi and Parvati. It matters

*From the *Guru Gita;* an accurate translation.

not if she has puffy cheeks or a nose like an owl's. When you hear that a zamindar is rich, you immediately infer that he is hand-some, virtuous, generous, and so on. Our Saria was only a village weaver's wife; you can of course draw your own conclusions about her.

Bhagia Chandra and Saria lived alone; there was no one else in their family. The village women say, "If a family has only a hus-band and a wife, the couple are free to go whenever and wherever they like." This might very well apply to our weaver couple. They had no worries and were very fond of each other. They did the housework together. When Bhagia wove clothes, Saria turned the spindles, prepared the thread, and put it on the wheel. When Saria cooked, Bhagia blew into the fireplace, kept the fire going, and fetched the water. Village humorists made fun of them in song:

Bhagia and Saria Chandra
A pair of village love-birds!

What wonderful poetry! But we believe that only the very fortu-nate in this world attract such mockery. Such people enjoy a bliss which, one imagines, exists only in heaven. An English poet once said, "People who experience pure marital bliss dwell in paradise, and they whose marital life is unhappy live in hell."

Oh, dear, we have made a terrible mistake! *Munīnāṃ ca mati-bhramaḥ*. Even sages commit blunders. In fact, sages habitually commit great errors in the course of their writing. Indeed, those who are distracted and commit errors while writing are called sages. Henceforth, people should address us as sage. What luck! We did not have to run like a mongoose around the Sahib throughout the year; neither did we get into debt trying to establish a hospital costing thousands of rupees; nor did we take the easy option of gaining the favor of the French by falling at their feet. And yet, without doing any of these things, we have received the title of sage. But, we never hesitate to sacrifice our self-interest if it means honoring the truth. *Na mithyā pātakam param.* No sin is greater than the sin of lying.* We believe that the wages of sin and falsehood stick to you; you can't pass them on to someone else. Thus, we feel compelled to write the truth, and nothing but the truth.

The truth is, Bhagia and Saria did not live all alone. There was one other member of their family living with them, a cow, named Neta. She was treated as a human being: Saria took care of Neta and cherished her like a daughter. The Lord of the universe has endowed mankind with a strange longing for children. Just as a starving man will devour leaves and twigs if he cannot find any food, a couple not blessed with children will have a pup or a kitten or a calf, and lavish all their affection on it. Saria spent nearly the whole day looking after Neta, and even when Neta was not tethered, she would stick close to Saria. If Neta ever went out of the yard into the village, Saria would call out, "Oh, my Neta!" and Neta would answer, "Ha . . . Ma," as if to say, "Yes mother," and run back to Saria and lick her all over. Saria, in turn, would caress her and talk to her sweetly about all manner of things. When Neta thrust her mouth into Saria's bowl of rice gruel, Saria would give her a soft tap and fondly scold her, "Naughty you." This mock anger, we know, was filled with joy and love. Bhagia, Saria, and Neta all slept in the same room, and Saria

---

*The translation is reasonably accurate, though the narrator deliberately distorts the grammar of the Sanskrit quote.

would leave a chaff and cow dung cake burning near Neta, to keep away fleas.

Neta was a perfect cow; and she had recently given birth to a calf. Her hide was black, and on her forehead was a white mark in the shape of the moon. It is said that a black cow with such markings belongs in a rich man's house. Neta's horns were narrow, strong, and close together; her tail was thin and long, with a thick tuft at the end, which swept the ground when she walked. Her back was curved and no wider than half a cubit. She had large haunches. A hump the size of a small squash graced her back, and from beneath her neck hung a dewlap longer than any other cow's. Her teats were as thick as ropes made of straw, and you can imagine the size of her udder. "Payodharībhūtacatuḥsamudrām."* Neta was not tall like a Kalinga cow; she was medium-sized. There is a proverb that says, "If a cow reaches your belly in height, eats a small quantity of chaff, but loves to eat green grass, it gives a lot of milk." It is said that milk is where a cow's mouth is. Does this mean you should put a vessel under the cow's mouth to milk her? No, it is not like that. A cow is like a paper mill. You feed rags, broken string, rotting weeds, and cotton in at one end of the mill, and from the other, you obtain clean, white, beautiful, smooth paper. Similarly, if you feed a cow chaff, rice gruel, and grass, milk will flow from her udder. We do not know how much milk Neta produced daily. But the other day she was the topic of discussion in Mangaraj's durbar. Everyone present agreed with one villager's estimate that Neta produced

*From Kalidasa's *Raghuvamsa*, where the fecund earth (which the dutiful king should protect) is seen metaphorically as a cow, whose teats are the oceans. Senapati is obviously transposing both context and meaning, using the passage from *Raghuvamsa* to refer to a real cow.

no fewer than five seers of milk a day. Mangaraj heaved a deep sigh and thought aloud, "What! That wretched weaver owns such a wonderful cow!"

People say, "Like father, like son." But they also say that a worthless son is born when a family faces ruin. Bhagia's father, Gobinda Chandra, was a worthy man. He was so highly respected in the neighboring villages that whenever a panchayat or village council was convened, he was asked to be a part of it. In times of trouble—the arrival of a court peon with a summons, or of an unstamped letter with postage due, to be collected from the addressee—no one dared come out until Gobinda came to the rescue. Gobinda did not, himself, weave clothes for a living; he collected clothes made by weavers and sold them in the market. Or, if a middleman came to the village, he would arrange to sell clothes to him. In doing so, he made a good profit. People were under the impression that Gobinda had made thousands. But we know that villagers are in the habit of exaggerating their own age and other people's wealth. Nonetheless, it is true that Gobinda did come by some money. When the fortunes of the family of Zamindar Bagha Singh began to decline, pieces of land were sold off. One of these, close by the village of Gobindapur, was purchased by Gobinda. It measured six and a third acres and was rent-free. There is a saying which goes, "A field made fertile by drainage water from a village always ends up in the hands of the village rent collector." In other words, the rent collector gets the best land. The piece of land Gobinda bought was watered by the village drains and so was very fertile. Since water was plentiful, it produced a rich harvest of rabana rice. They say, "If you have good land, plant only rabana; it will grow cubit-long ears, and be the envy of your neighbor." Flood or drought, the land yielded eight bharanas of grain per acre. But, Bhagia was a weaver, what did he know about farming? He gave it out to sharecroppers and received only about five bharanas per acre.

Although Bhagia was simple-minded, he nevertheless had a number of good qualities. On occasions such as death anniversaries, nabanna, the new rice festival, he would feast his fellow weavers; never did a wandering singer or beggar leave his door empty-handed. Simple-minded people have no enemies. Bhagia and Saria did not take part in village gossip; whenever a quarrel broke out in the village, they withdrew into their house and bolted the door. Everyone liked them. We believe that need lies at the root of all misery; people suffer if they are denied any desirable, coveted, or basic things such as wealth, learning, fame, health, and so on. Our weaver couple lacked for nothing. If you wished to see, reunited in one place, such heavenly qualities as devoted love between husband and wife, holiness of affection, absolute bliss, unfailing physical well-being, and simple piety, we would direct you to their abode. From our long experience and our great learning, we know that fate has denied mankind the enjoyment of uninterrupted bliss. How then did the weaver couple escape this heavenly decree? The great poet Kalidasa says, "God is averse to creating a human being who is blessed with all the joys of life." How can we ignore this wise saying?

Is the weaver couple really happy? One cannot know if a salagram stone is standing or lying on its side. Human feelings are expressed in tears or smiles, but no one has ever seen this couple smiling or heard them crying. If they talked, we might perhaps know, but they rarely talked to anyone in the village. No one, however, can hide anything from us. Just as hunters follow the trail of an animal to track it down, so too do we follow the activities of human beings to figure out what is going on in their minds. The other night, for instance, Saria went out to attend the sixth-day celebrations of Rukuni Ma's daughter-in-law's child. She came away after the rice cakes were distributed to the guests. On reaching home, she went straight to bed, complaining of a stomachache. We also know that, until very late at night, she lay awake, tossing and turning in bed. Bhagia tried to console her saying, "God has not given us what we want. Why pine for it?"

It is not clear from this what Saria was pining for. These days Saria kept herself busy observing all sorts of religious rites. Her worship of the goddess Budhi Mangala was becoming more and more ardent. Usually, if you see someone at the door of a lawyer or a doctor, you know that some calamity has befallen them. Well, the goddess Budhi Mangala was both a doctor and a lawyer. She was very useful whenever someone in the village fell sick or was involved in a court case. Saria's intense devotion to Budhi Mangala leads us to suspect that some hidden grief was eating her away. In the middle of working her spindles, on the verandah, she would stop whenever her eyes fell on a little child playing in the village path. On festive occasions such as the new moon or the full moon, she would heave a deep sigh and look at the cakes and sweetmeats she herself had prepared. It took a lot of persuasion on Bhagia's part to make her eat a little of these. The other day someone asked Bhagia to weave a piece of cloth for a child. After the cloth was woven, Saria took a long time folding it, and Bhagia gave a deep sigh when he saw her eyes brimming with tears.

CHAPTER ELEVEN

Gobara Jena, the Chowkidar

The Dom quarter, some four or five hundred steps from where the weavers lived, was surrounded by rice fields. It was not a separate village; it formed part of Gobindapur. There lived ten Dom families and Gobara Jena, the village chowkidar. For his services, he received an acre and a half of land. In addition, at harvest time he collected one sheaf of corn from every house in the village. Accepting bribes came naturally to Jena, but it must be admitted that he was a competent and clever chowkidar. No thefts occurred in the village because of him. True, there were four or five burglaries every year, but Jena, the bribe taker, could not be held responsible for them; they occurred on nights when he was four or five miles away in another village, attending caste rituals. Jena, the chowkidar, walked his beat in the village throughout the night, but was so effective that no one felt his presence. See, the point is, if he shouted while on his beat, the thieves would take fright and run away, and even then he would not be able to catch them.

It is said that in olden days, the police were great bribe takers. Only Lord Jagannath could say if this is true. People should be gagged and stopped from spreading rumors. Tigers eat men, but does that mean all tigers are man-eaters? Surely, it is possible to find honest and virtuous tigers. Our Jena was an honest and virtuous man. He accepted sheaves of corn from the villagers as his due every year, a length of coarse homespun cloth when a marriage took place, and from the bridegroom he received the customary gift of one rupee. On top of all this, when there was an unnatural death in the village, he would extort a bribe, and, occasionally, he would help himself to a pumpkin or squash from someone's garden. That was all! No one could say he was greedy. Of course, he charged one rupee whenever he was asked to file a report at the police station about a theft, a snakebite, a drowning, or whatever. You must agree that there was nothing illegal about this charge. We would rather say that Gobardhan was a kindhearted man. If a poor man found himself on the wrong side of the law, our Gobardhan would take only a piece of bronze or a bell-metal utensil from him, and not charge the poor fellow a paisa. It was also to be expected that he should take from the village a bunch of bananas, some pumpkins or squash for the munshi, the darogas, and the constables at the police station, which he visited every month. The pressure of his work was such that he had no time to eat his evening meal in his own house; the villagers, therefore, had to take turns feeding him. Before darkness fell, he would tell his host-for-the-night not to forget to cook an extra handful of rice for him. If, for some reason, his host happened to forget, then that same night the chowkidar would happen to forget to keep watch over his house. Somehow, thieves knew of this immediately, and that very night they would carry off some fruit or grain. If they failed to find anything worth stealing, they would pull down one of the verandah's pillars.

After finishing his evening meal, Jena would head for home, shouting along the way, "Beware, Beware!" His shouts would send children who were still awake to bed. After that, no one could say whether he walked his beat throughout the night.

Although Gobara Jena was a Pana by caste, he was no ordinary Pana. He was rich: if he so wanted, he could easily produce a thousand rupees. Five to seven bharanas of grain were stored at his house. However, no matter how clever one is, one cannot always escape bad times. Once, even he, Gobara Jena, came close to being convicted in a case of theft. It is said that he got out of it by slipping 250 rupees to the munshi. It happened that eight dacoits were arrested in connection with a burglary committed in the house of Bhubani Sha, a moneylender and oil merchant in Makhanpur. One of the accused, a worthless Pana, confessed that the burglary, and ten to fifteen others, had been carried out with the connivance of Gobara Jena, who had also helped sell off the stolen goods. Since the other person accused did not support this Pana's story, Gobara escaped unscathed.

Mangaraj was very pleased with Gobara, for Gobara was an able man. Every morning and every evening he was to be found at Mangaraj's kacheri. Mangaraj and Gobara were often seen sitting together, alone, in the dead of night. Now, a number of Panas lived in the zamindari of Fatepur Sarsandha: it was suspected that they were involved in thefts, dacoities, and waylaying travelers. This suspicion was based on knowledge of the number of times the police visited the Panas, and the Panas visited the prison. Our Gobardhan had one great quality: if a Pana was jailed, he looked after his helpless family members. He arranged for them to have supplies of grain from Mangaraj's store. Detractors, however, always remain detractors; these people never stopped bad-mouthing Jena. They attached a very different meaning to this good trait of Gobardhan's and cast aspersions on Mangaraj's charity toward the Panas' families.

CHAPTER TWELVE

Asura Pond

There was only one pond in Gobindapur, and everyone in the village used it. It was fairly large, covering ten to twelve batis, with banks ten to twelve arm-lengths high, and was known as Asura Pond. In the middle once stood sixteen stone pillars, on which lamps were lighted. We are unable to recount the true story of who had it dug, or when. It is said that demons, the Asuras, dug it themselves. That could well be true. Could humans like us dig such an immense pond? Here is a brief history of Asura Pond, as told to us by Ekadusia, the ninety-five-year-old weaver.

The demon Banasura ordered that the pond be dug, but did not pick up shovels and baskets to dig it himself. On his orders, a host of demons came one night and did the work. But when day broke, it had not yet been completed: there was a gap of twelve to fourteen arm-lengths in the south bank, which had not been filled in. By now, it was morning, and the villagers were already up and about. Where could the demons go? They dug a tunnel connecting the pond to the banks of the River Ganga, escaped through it, bathed in the holy river, and then disappeared. During the Baruni Festival on the Ganga, the holy waters of the river used to gush through the tunnel into the pond. But, as the villagers became sinful, the river no longer did this. English-educated babus, do not be too critical of our local historian, Ekadusia Chandra. If you are, half of what Marshman and Tod have written will not survive the light of scrutiny.

There were fish in the pond. You might well remark, "Of course, where there is water, there are fish. There is little need to note this." But your objection is not, strictly speaking, logical. Although sugarcane and jaggery, body and bone, always go together, there exists no such necessary relation between water and fish. If there did, you would find fish inside the water pitchers in your houses. It is not in our nature to base what we write on vague guesswork. We shall provide irrefutable proof that there were fish in Asura Pond. Consider, if you will, the three long-beaked crocodiles lying immobile, with their mouths open, on the south side of the pond. They were there every day. Why were they in the pond? What did they live on? Did anyone see them grazing in the fields like cattle? Or did they follow the path of nonviolence, like the Jains? Needless to say, since they were alive, they must have been eating something. What could this "something" have been? Long-beaked crocodiles are also known as fish-eating crocodiles. Someone might contend, "True, they were eating fish, but they could very well have been getting fish from somewhere else." Of course, fresh and salted fish were in fact sold in the market, but no one ever saw the crocodiles carrying money and going there. When the fisherwomen come to the village to sell fish, village women gave them rice in exchange. But we can swear under oath that we never saw crocodiles obtaining fish in exchange for rice. Thus, it is proven beyond doubt that there were fish in Asura Pond.

There is another equally irrefutable proof to support this contention. Look over there! Four kaduakhumpi birds are hopping about like gotipuas, like traditional dancing boys. The birds are happy and excited because they are able to spear and eat the little fish that live in the mud. Some might remark that these birds are so cruel, so wicked, that they get pleasure from spearing and eating creatures smaller than themselves! What can we say? You may describe the kaduakhumpi birds as cruel, wicked, satanic, or whatever else you like; the birds will never file a defamation suit against you. But don't you know that among your fellow human beings, the bravery, honor, respectability, indeed, the attractiveness of an individual all depend upon the number of necks he can wring?

Some sixteen to twenty cranes, white and brown, churn the mud like lowly farmhands, from morning till night. This is the third proof that there are fish in the pond. A pair of kingfishers suddenly arrive out of nowhere, dive into the water a couple of times, stuff themselves with food, and swiftly fly away. Sitting on the bank, a lone kingfisher suns itself, wings spread like the gown of a memsahib. Oh, stupid Hindu cranes, look at these English kingfishers, who arrive out of nowhere with empty pockets, fill themselves with all manner of fish from the pond, and then fly away. You nest in the banyan tree near the pond, but after churning the mud and water all day long, all you get are a few miserable small fish. You are living in critical times now; more and more kingfishers will swoop down on the pond and carry off the best fish. You have no hope, no future, unless you go abroad and learn how to swim in the ocean.

The kite is smart and clever; it perches quietly on a branch, like a Brahmin guru, and from there swoops down into the pond to snatch a big fish. That lasts it for the whole day. Brahmin gurus perch on their verandahs, descending on their disciples once a year, like the kite.

Forty or fifty arm-lengths from where the cranes were feeding, the pond is covered with water hyacinths and various kinds of creepers and plants. In the midst of these, water lilies, like young Hindu daughters-in-law, blossom at night; during the day they fold themselves in and hide their faces from view. But the water hyacinths, like young unmarried girls, gaily toss their heads about, day and night, without shame, without a care in the world. The ratalilies bloom at a further distance in the pond. They are like educated Christian "ladies"; they have parted company with the water lilies, but have not yet joined the lotuses.

In the middle of the pond, no water hyacinths are to be found, because goddess Budhi Mangala visits this part of the pond every night. The lotus flower is the darling of Indian poets; it is the abode of Lakshmi, the goddess of wealth, and the seat of Saraswati, the goddess of learning. Furthermore, Lord Brahma's birthplace is graced with lotuses. So naturally, in our village goddess Budhi Mangala has the monopoly on this holy and beautiful flower. Once a villager swam out into the pond to pluck a lotus. The goddess got his feet entangled with creepers, dragged him down, and drowned him. Since that day, no one has dared to even glance at the lotus flowers in the pond.

There were four bathing ghats in Asura Pond, but only three

were used. No one went to the ghat on the south side of the pond, except when someone died and funeral rites were performed. This ghat was a frightening place; even during the day, you would find no one there. And who would venture there at night? Close by grew a large aswatha tree, where, as everyone knows, two terrible demons lived. They were often seen sitting in the tree at night, stretching their legs out into the middle of the pond. We do not know the names of the persons who had seen these demons, but the story is nevertheless true. There were also eyewitness accounts of several kinds of ghosts, who fished in the pond, especially on dark rainy nights, lighting fires here and there. The washerman's ghat was on the east side; two washermen were busy washing clothes. It is said that you know if a village is neat or untidy by looking at its washerman's ghat. Cartloads of dirty clothes were piled up like sacks, and four washerwomen were engaged in boiling and drying clothes. The weavers' ghat was at the northwest corner of the pond; women gathered there in large numbers, since it was close to the village, giving it the look of a haat, a country market. Just because we have used the word *haat*, do not for a moment think that things were bought and sold there; we call it a haat because there were a lot of people, producing a great deal of noise. The gathering at the ghat became very large when the women came to bathe before cooking their daytime meals. If there had been a daily newspaper in Gobindapur, its editor would have had no difficulty gathering stories for his paper; all he would have had to do was sit at the ghat, paper and pencil in hand. He would have found out, for instance, what had been cooked the previous night, at whose house, and what was going to be cooked there today; who went to sleep at what time; how many mosquitoes bit whom; who ran out of salt; who had borrowed oil from whom; how Rama's mother's young daughter-in-law was a shrew, and how she talked back to her mother-in-law, although she married only the other day; when Kamali would go back to her in-laws; how Saraswati was a nice girl and how her cooking was good, her manners excellent . . .

Padi started a brief lecture as she sat in the water cleaning her teeth. The sum and substance of it was that no one in the village was a better cook than she. She went on tirelessly, pouring out much relevant and irrelevant information. A few pretty women went on rubbing their faces with their sari ends, in order to look even prettier. Lakshmi's nose, adorned with a nose jewel, had already become red from too much rubbing. Sitting at the water's edge, scrubbing her heavy brass armlets with half a basketful of sand, Bimali was engaged in a long tirade against some unnamed person, using words not to be found in any dictionary. The gist of it was that somebody's cow had eaten her pumpkin creepers last night. Bimali proceeded to offer some stinking stuff as food to three generations of the cow owner's ancestors, going on and on about the fertile soil in her back garden: the wretched cow had not merely devoured the shiny pumpkins that grew there but had destroyed the possibility of it producing many more such delicious pumpkins. With the help of several cogent arguments and examples, she also demonstrated that this cow must be given as a gift to a Brahmin, otherwise a terrible calamity would befall the owner. If a violent quarrel between Markandia's mother and Jasoda had not suddenly erupted and put an end to all the talk, we could have gathered many more such items of news.

Jasoda was sitting in the water cleaning her teeth. Markandia, a five-year-old boy, who was jumping about and muddying the water, happened to splatter her. Jasoda stood up, screamed at the boy in foul language, and cursed him with a short life—whereupon Markandia's mother rushed in and shouted back at Jasoda in matching language. In the end, Markandia's mother was vanquished; she slapped her son, picked up her pitcher, and, grabbing Markandia's hand, retreated resentfully. Markandia began to howl, baring all his teeth, and on this note the great battle at the ghat ended.

The sound of thunder lingers long after lightning flashes. The quarrel was over, but talk about it continued. The middle-aged women formed one group and the older women another, one group siding with Markandia's mother and the other with Jasoda. For our part, we are entirely behind Jasoda. After long deliberation and rigorous analysis we have come to the conclusion that Markandia was the cause of all the trouble. He was definitely the villain; his crime was unpardonable. You may scold him, thrash him, or do whatever you like with him—we will stand by you. After all, as you know, water is life, and everyone used water from the weavers' ghat for drinking. Markandia dirtied this water. Would you consider this a small crime?

Now about twenty women arrived at the ghat to bathe. They all stepped into the pond, sat down, and started cleaning their teeth. Milk-white spittle from their mouths floated about in the pond, along with the bits of reddish stuff they scraped off their tongues. We hesitate to describe what else was floating there, since all the women had just relieved themselves in the nearby fields. Even Jasoda would admit she herself had done the same. It is a time-honored practice, not a crime, and therefore there is no reason why it should not be written. Once someone joked that for every pitcherful of water women carried from the pond they discharged a quarter back into it. That may be true, but we have no way of verifying it. More women, carrying bed linens, arrived and began washing them in the ghat; some washed their children's dirty clothing in the water. But, we are sure none of them made the water filthy by jumping about in it, like Markandia had. Unless you do that, how can the water become dirty? Therefore, considering all this evidence, we conclude that Markandia's crime was definitely of a very serious nature.

The Saanta ghat lay three hundred steps away from the weavers' ghat. No women went there in the morning; it was used only by men. During the month of Baisakha it seems as if the sky rains down embers; a hot wind blows and scorches the skin. The dust from the fields rises like smoke from a fire. There was now a crowd of men at the ghat. The farmers, who had gone out to plough the fields in the small hours of the night, had now unyoked their bullocks. Some had come to the ghat after leaning their ploughs against the walls and rubbing a little oil on their heads and bodies. Others had come with a two-finger-thick towel, starched with rice gruel, thrown over their shoulders. Some did not even have a towel; they came straight to the pond from the fields, unyoked their bullocks at the ghat, and stepped into the water. A few pairs of bullocks grazed nearby after drinking all the water they wanted from the pond. Some bathers went into the pond chewing their toothsticks; they cleaned their teeth, scraped their tongues, and threw the dirty sticks on the bank. Half a cartload of dried toothsticks lay there in a heap.

It was not as if the men were silent while they bathed. No, like the women, they too talked a lot. But their talk was repetitive, always centering on the same themes. Therefore, there is no point reporting at length what they talked about. They usually discussed matters like these: how much land had been sown and where; which field had been ploughed for the second time; how Rama performed the sowing ceremony; how quick-footed Bhima's bullocks were; how the zamindar's were no ordinary bullocks, but truly two young elephants; how X had foolishly wasted a lot of money on a pair of useless brown bullocks; that this was the month when grain would be loaned out from the zamindar's granary; that the monsoon was expected in fifteen days' time; and that the astrologer had predicted plenty of rain this year. But these are familiar subjects. It is not necessary to elaborate on them here.

CHAPTER THIRTEEN

Words of Wisdom

"Why this whispering?" asked the first woman.
"A house will be ruined," replied the second.
"A farm or a house?"
"All things will come to an end."

How wonderful! Philosophy at the weavers' ghat!

The women who had come to bathe before cooking the midday meal had all gone home. Only two middle-aged women remained behind, engaged in the above conversation while cleaning their teeth. They exchanged knowing glances, smiled, then suddenly fell silent, as if sensing danger.

Talk loudly and no one will bother about what you say; even people standing close to you will behave as if they have not heard. But let two people whisper to each other, and everyone will be dying to find out what is going on. Just as a big tree is hidden in a small seed, a great event lies concealed in a whispered word. There was no one else around. Why were these two middle-aged women talking in whispers? Why did they suddenly become quiet?

A banyan tree and an aswatha tree grew close together to the right of the weavers' ghat, some twenty arm-lengths from where the steps led down to the water's edge. Both trees were young and healthy, and loaded with tender leaves. People believe that if you unite a banyan tree and an aswatha tree near a ghat or a road, you will earn as much merit as you would by giving away a daughter in marriage. Such married trees, symbolizing a Hindu custom, are found in many places.

Over the course of their conversation, the two women glanced a few times toward the trees near the ghat. Did they think they could conceal anything from us? Thieves wait until the dead of night to steal, yet the jails are crowded with convicted robbers. You cannot throw dust into the eyes of a smart and clever detective. A definite connection existed between the base of the trees and the conversation between these two women. See, our inference was absolutely sound! Just as an expert weaver can disentangle a skein once he gets hold of the main thread, so too we can tell a story, if you just give us a lead. Behind the banyan and the aswatha trees, sat two women, huddled together, talking about something. We both know them well. What were they doing there, at such an unusual hour, in such an unlikely place? It was a meeting of opposites: a wily, wicked she-jackal, and a simple, innocent ewe. The former poured forth a stream of words, her jeweled nose turned up, her watchful face poised like a snake's hood. The latter had a pitcher placed near her; in her right hand, she held a bunch of toothsticks; and her forehead was covered with the end of her sari. She kept staring at the former like a ewe stunned by some terrible sound. Just as King Parikshit listened with a pure heart and a calm mind, to the Puranas from the sage, Sukadev, she imbibed the words pouring forth from the other woman. But, we cannot say if the words sank into her mind or merely passed through her ears.

We have no doubt that you would like to know what the women were talking about. A drunkard once said, "The world is a poisonous tree, bearing only two fruits that taste like nectar: one is wine, the other is meat." On hearing this old man, Manu retorted that only ghosts or ghostlike people say such things. We agree. The old are never wrong, as they say. Nevertheless, the poisonous tree—better known as the world—bears two nectar-sweet fruit. We know them only by their names. Since it is our duty to do good deeds, we will tell you the names, for your benefit: the first is Desire-to-listen-to-whispered-words; the second, Desire-to-malign-others. Whisper someone's family secrets, or speak evil of someone, and people will quickly give you their complete attention. See how sweet these two fruits are?

We started writing about one thing and now we are writing about something else! No matter how well you row a boat, the current pulls it away from its destination. But a strong and able helmsman keeps the boat on a steady course. True, our pen moves helter-skelter, but our main story never loses its way; it is always on course.

Anyway, it is quite unfair of us to keep you guessing any longer; we must now tell you, clearly and without ambiguity, who the two women huddled together near the trees were, and what passed between them. Some people provide a long preface, and give a long lecture before they tell you anything; but our nature is not at all like that. We waste no time in saying what we have to say. Also, some people hide things, out of fear, and blurt out others they hadn't originally planned to say. Remember how the two middle-aged women suddenly fell silent while they were talking in gestures? But we are braver than those weaver women; we will tell you everything, with heroic fearlessness. In fact, we are otherwise very unimportant; so much so that if we shouted for help, no one would come to our rescue. But, if an important person merely yawns, a crowd of two hundred people will gather just to watch. People in Britain even pay money to be present when important persons open their mouths!

The two women sitting near the banyan and aswatha trees were well known in the village. You too know them. Human beings are known not by their faces, but by their characters; one's fame depends on how people talk about one's character, whether it is good or bad. Of course, many women lived in the village of Gobindapur; but these two stood out: one for her wily and wicked nature, the other for her simplicity and innocence. When such different, but equally well-known women confer in secret, it is hard to wait to find out what they discussed.

We have sat down to write all this only in order to satisfy your curiosity, and much hard work and care have gone into collecting all the details. One of them delivered a very long speech. There may be a few things in it not entirely to your taste. Since we are unused to writing long drawn-out narratives, we will give you only the sum and substance of it.

"Look, Saria, Goddess Budhi Mangala is the cause of everything that happens in this world. All creatures obey her. Life in the world depends on her wishes. Can her commands ever be disobeyed? After so much worship, and so much fasting, you are extremely fortunate to have received her command. In the past, it was the zamindar's family that the goddess favored. Now she has bestowed her favors on you. All you have to do is to build her a temple, and you will see how your house will be filled with wealth. Lots and lots of money will come pouring in, from everywhere; you will have rows upon rows of grain sacks stacked in your house. After that, your husband, Bhagavan, will no longer have to weave clothes for a living. Ten maidservants will be at your beck and call. All you have to do is obey Goddess Budhi Mangala's command. Somehow, you must get the temple built. Why worry about the money? Who would not loan you money, once Budhi Mangala's command has become known? And you don't have to go anywhere else, not even in the dead of the night. Ramachandra Mangaraj will lend you the money. I will take it upon myself to arrange the loan; you don't have to do anything. Building a temple will not cost much: only one hundred and fifty rupees. With that, a big temple can be raised, as tall and as wide as the Baladev Temple in Kendrapada. Just mortgage your six and a third acres to Mangaraj, and I will get you the money. Don't think anyone is going to snatch your land away; it will be exactly where it has always been. The only difference is that there will be some writing on a piece of paper. Once the temple is built, you will be so rich that you yourself will give loans to other people. I am sure the goddess has already given you a token. A gold coin, no doubt. Can you imagine the goddess giving a silver coin as a token?"

It is difficult for us to believe that Saria understood anything of this lengthy speech. Indeed, she was completely baffled. She kept staring at the face of the woman delivering the lecture. How could she, of all people, make sense of such a huge sum of money? Even with a few coins worth just one rupee, Saria would go indoors, close the door, and she and Bhagia would spend three hours counting it out correctly. Whenever Bhagia's earnings for the day exceeded one rupee, Saria would have her brother,

Lokanthia, count the coins. Also she could not decide if the presence of five or six maids in her house would be a blessing or a disaster. What a dilemma! She wished her husband, Bhagia, were with her. She also wanted to get away from this place. She heaved a deep sigh, looked at her pitcher, uttering only, "My good Mistress Champa." Then she became quiet. She had nothing else to add. But wily Champa understood; she realized her tricks were having no effect on her prey, and the prey was now struggling to break free and escape. After much time and effort the cat had finally caught a hilsa fish. How could she allow it to slip out of her jaws? She must try a new strategy.

Champa said, "Look, Saria, what good are money and gold? They do not help us go to heaven. The only wealth in life is children. A house without a child is dark even at midday. Do you think being barren is merely a small sin? The *Bhagavata* is recited in the zamindar's house, and I listen to it every day. The other day the priest read these lines from the sacred book:

Avoid the face of a barren woman in the morning;
Virtuous is the woman who has borne three sons.

A barren woman is a disgrace to her village;
A woman without a child suffers greatly in this world.

Does the *Bhagavata* mislead us? Is it for nothing that everyone bows before the wooden seat on which the *Bhagavata* is kept? Haven't you noticed that no one ever walks past your house? Why? Because no one wants to see your face at the auspicious hour. You must have heard that the zamindar's wife herself was barren and that we never looked at her face until well past the first hour of the day. She felt wretched and miserable, and so she offered prayers to Goddess Mangala. The goddess bestowed her kindness on the zamindar's wife, and now she has shown you her mercy. And you know the zamindar's wife has become a grandmother."

Saria began to daydream. Her ears started to buzz. She wanted to run away, but felt unable to move. The cat had at last pounced. Tears welled up in Saria's eyes. She wanted to say something, but was struck dumb. With great effort, she opened her mouth.

"Whatever shall I do?" she asked. "People say that once land is mortgaged to the zamindar it never returns to its owner."

"Oh, Ram! Oh, Ram!" exclaimed Champa. "How could you say such a thing! How could the zamindar take your land, when he is lending you the money to honor Goddess Budhi Mangala? Why do you listen to what the villagers say? Gobindapur is the wickedest place on earth. The women of this village would murder you in broad daylight. Seeing you so prosperous, they are dying of envy. People are so jealous here that a man who eats one meal a day cannot stand a man who eats two. Don't say anything to anyone. What's more, those who don't obey the goddess's command go blind and deaf, and then die. Don't you know that three women in Gopinathpur lost their husbands at the same time because they had disobeyed the goddess's command?"

Saria was listening to Champa quietly, so quietly that she might as well have been a wooden puppet. But Champa's last words were too much for her. She burst into tears. Shaking and sobbing, she asked, "What shall I do? What ever shall I do?" Clever Champa now realized that she had at last hit her target. She was convinced her strategy had worked. Elated, she said, "Look Saria, you have nothing to fear. You don't have to do anything. Leave everything to me."

"I need nothing. All I want is for my husband to stay safe and well," said Saria.

"Don't be afraid for him. He'll be safe."

Then Champa placed the garland of Lord Dadhibaman and some holy prasad in Saria's hand, and said, "As this is my witness, I will make sure that all shall be well. You shall be blessed with three sons, and your husband Bhagavan will live for centuries. Don't worry at all."

"What shall I do? Oh, Mistress Champa? What shall I do?" cried Saria.

"You will have to do nothing," replied Champa. "Both Bhagavan and you must come here this evening. Then, I will do what is necessary. Once you undertake to carry out Goddess Mangala's command, you will have to fast or eat only a few rice flakes until the work is completed. I am telling you all this because you know nothing about performing these sacred rites."

After this, Saria made her way toward the ghat to take her bath. Champa stayed on for a while near the trees, looked around contentedly, then headed for the zamindar's house.

After careful investigation we have learned that Saria was in the zamindar's house, and Bhagavan with her, until midnight. Then, nobody saw Bhagavan in the village for the next four days; some said they had seen him on the road to Cuttack.

CHAPTER FOURTEEN

The Conspiracy

Hear the jackals? It must be midnight. Even though there are no clocks in Gobindapur, the villagers know what time it is when they hear the howling. Animals can serve many useful functions in a village. When there is no municipal commissioner, jackals are responsible for clearing away the carcasses of dogs, rats, cats, and other unclean animals.

It was now midnight. All was quiet; not a sound could be heard from any quarter. A while ago a baby in a house in the oil-men's lane began to cry. Sleepily, the mother patted him, promising him rare and precious things if he went back to sleep, warning him that terrible creatures—thieves, chowkidars, tigers—were on their way. She caressed him, told him what a nice baby he was, and then they both fell asleep. In the courtyard of Mangaraj's kacheri, Gobara Jena and Sautunia, the chowkidar from the next village, were fast asleep by two small fires, which kept away the mosquitoes. Two long bamboo lathis were at their sides. Listening to their snoring a passerby might have thought pigs were feeding in the courtyard. Although we are very careful and always thoroughly investigate before reaching a conclusion, we ourselves were of that opinion for a while. But when we pricked up our ears and listened carefully, we discovered why even we mistook them for pigs. Three tenant farmers tossed and turned on the outer verandah of the kacheri, slapping themselves in their sleep to drive away the mosquitoes. As you know, hunger, worry, and mosquitoes are the enemies of sleep. These three farmers had not been allowed to go home because they had not paid back the grain they had borrowed from the zamindar. They had not been given any food all day, and now they were being tormented by mosquitoes. And, to top it all off, their worries kept haunting them. How could they sleep?

Next to the kacheri wing was Mangaraj's bedroom. People called it the treasury. Of all the rooms in the house, it was the finest, as it should well have been. It faced east; it had five beams supporting the roof, an atoo ceiling and a wide verandah. Its two-winged door was made from the strong wood of the jack-fruit tree; on it were square carvings and iron knobs. An iron ring and chain, with two large pipe-shaped padlocks, were fitted onto it. A very narrow window with iron bars was set waist-high into the west wall. This window was always kept closed, except on Thursdays during the month of Margasira, when the room had to be cleaned. The room was very dark; even in the daytime, a lamp was needed. In the corners, cockroaches and rats vied for supremacy. Champa perhaps felt a certain fondness for the cockroaches: she and they had the same complexion. She used to say that cockroaches were auspicious because they brought wealth. For this reason, generations of cockroaches were allowed to infest the room. A long bamboo bench rested against the north wall, and on it were three large, old cane baskets. Near the bench lay a plank-bed. On the floor, in one corner, were pots containing jaggery, pickled mangoes, and a few cans of karanj oil. There was no need for Mangarj to buy oil from the market. Loads of karanj seeds were brought from the groves in the outlying villages of the zamindari, and the oilman, one of the zamindar's bonded laborers, pressed the seeds for free. The oil was then stored in Mangaraj's bedroom. Two heavy boxes made from the wood of a mango tree stood close to a large sal-wood box. This was said to belong to Lakshmi, the goddess of wealth. Every evening Champa lighted a cotton wick near it and worshipped it. Every Thursday a puja was performed near it, with vermilion and sandal paste, and offerings of fine rice and jaggery were made to the goddess. From one of the beams supporting the ceiling hung three or four pots of ghee. Every day, every cowherd in the zamindari had to send ghee to the zamindar's house.

Cobwebs covered the ropes and beams, hanging like silken tassels inside a palanquin. Mangaraj's bed was placed against the west wall of the room: one end facing south and the other north. On the south end there was a huge pillow. The bed had a grass mattress covered with a thick cotton quilt. At first glance the quilt looked like a piece of exquisitely dotted fabric; on close inspection, however, the reddish-black spots proved to be blood shed by myriad martyred bedbugs.

Tonight, in this room, a man and a woman were deep in conversation; the man was seated on the bed, the woman, on the floor. Our readers will recognize them: the woman was Champa, and the man was no other than our Ramachandra Mangaraj. Champa had both hands placed firmly on the edge of the bed, and Mangaraj was leaning slightly toward her. A brass lamp stand stood three arm-lengths from the bed, and on it, a clay lamp burned feebly. The lamp stand was covered with oil stains; a small quantity of bluish oil, mixed with burned wick ends, had collected in the plate at its base.

Perhaps you would not like to hear what was going on between Champa and Mangaraj, and what dark conspiracies they were hatching together. We normally do not write more than is strictly required. Yet, whether you consider our narrative to be true or a mere novel or romance, it just won't do for us to neglect to write about our hero and our heroine. Therefore, we will have to satisfy demands from all quarters, and have our cake and eat a bit of it, too.

"That bastard, of unknown father, of unknown mother!" began Champa. "He lets his cows loose in other people's fields, destroys their crops and when I complain, the bastard abuses me! May he die an early death. If he didn't have a lathi, I tell you my Lord, I would've bitten off his nose! Oh, I almost fainted from fear when I saw his lathi! You must do something about him. Unless you teach him a lesson, I will knock my brains out or drink poison or drown myself." Having said this she began to sob.

"Champa, calm down," said Mangaraj. "I too am scared of his lathi. He and his brothers are stupid ruffians; they raise their lathis at the slightest provocation. I would have taught them a lesson long ago, but they are so watchful even our cats cannot enter their village. Our Gobara is very clever and careful; yet, even he hasn't been able to do anything. After all, what could he do? They have guards posted both day and night."

"No, no, my lord, you must not give up," cried Champa. "You must do something. Otherwise I will lose face before the women of this village. Are they so mighty they can defeat even you?"

"Look Champa, the Shastras advise us, 'Get the better of the enemy through brute force, deceit, or guile.' Though I have failed, you can certainly find a way. If you put your mind to it, something could be done. For three years, I had tried to trap that weaver, Bhagia; but as soon as you took the matter into your own hands, the deed was done."

Champa pushed up the burning wick in the lamp, then burst out laughing, very pleased with herself. "At first I thought I wouldn't be able to do it. But, what can't we do if we use our wits? Aren't you sending the farmhands, tomorrow, to plough Bhagia's six acres and a third?"

"I've already told the farmhands to take the plough to Bhagia's field tomorrow. I'll go there myself."

"You did the right thing pulling down Bhagia and Saria's house. If you had left it standing, they would certainly have created trouble for us later."

"Well," said Mangaraj. "The land had been mortgaged to me for a period of six months. Since they couldn't repay the loan on time, I took their land. And, the house was auctioned off to meet the court costs. I bid for it, got it, and pulled it down."

"I didn't really want their piece of land, or their house," said Champa. "What I had my heart set on was their cow; that's why I went to so much trouble. She is no ordinary cow, but a regular young elephant. I have left her tethered on the verandah. To-morrow she will be taken into our cowshed. Where did the wretched couple go?"

"Which couple? Oh, you mean Bhagia and Saria? They have nowhere to go, and now they wander from door to door like un-appeased ghosts."

"The other day, I found Saria beating her head and wailing before Goddess Budhi Mangala. When she saw me, she wept all the more bitterly and came toward me as if to say something. But I looked away, and left."

After this Champa and Mangaraj had a long discussion that lasted until midnight. It gradually became so guarded and secretive that we were unable to listen in on them to make our report. We do know that they were looking at each other intently, totally absorbed in their conversation, when the shadow of a woman fell between them. Startled, they looked up and noticed a silent figure. They suddenly fell quiet. The woman heaved a deep sigh, such as one lets out when a deep sorrow burdens the soul. No one uttered a word, or stirred; they were like wooden statues. Everything seemed still.

After a few moments, Mangaraj looked up at the woman and asked, "What's the matter?" There was no answer. Mangaraj demanded, "What's the matter?" The woman did not reply, only sighing deeply once again. Annoyed, Mangaraj raised his voice and repeated, "What's the matter? Why don't you speak?"

The Saantani, for the woman was no other than Mangaraj's wife, said softly, "It's already very late. You should retire to bed. Don't stay here planning other people's ruin."

A disrespectful grunt was Champa's reply.

"Well, you go. I'll join you later," said Mangaraj to the Saantani.

Champa's grunt pierced the Saantani's heart like a spear, and Mangaraj's words, "You go," stung her like a million scorpions. "Champa is to stay, and I am to leave!"

A tender-hearted woman can endure sorrows which would break a tough man's heart. A woman's capacity for tolerance is greater than that of any man, but no pure and chaste woman can bear her husband's scorn and lack of trust. For her, to be slighted in her husband's presence by a maidservant was worse than death. But this was nothing new; the Saantani had got used to this kind of humiliation. Even then, tears choked her, and her limbs became numb. Somehow, she collected herself, walked out, leaned against a wall. Then, suddenly she sank to the ground. We have been told that after that night no one heard a word escape her lips. People often saw tears in her eyes, although she tried her best to hold them back.

Slamming the door shut, Champa returned to her seat, saying, "I don't feel hurt if someone abuses me or gives me a beating with a broomstick, but my heart bleeds if someone utters even one word against you. Didn't you hear what the Saantani just said? No husband should want to look at her face after hearing that. She knows everything about Saria's land. What more does she want to know? Saria's problems worried us for a year. A lot of money went out of this house; a lot of money was spent in law courts in Cuttack. You sent ten or twenty cartloads of stone for the temple Saria was to build for Goddess Mangala. And after all that, the Saantani wants us to return the six and a third acres to Saria, and asks us not to pull her house down as well."

Champa broke into peals of laughter, which peirced the stillness of the night. This laughter could not have failed to reach the Saantani's ears, but she was too numb to feel anything. What passed between Champa and Mangaraj that night is not known to anyone. One only overheard Champa saying, "You give me a palanquin, five loads of gifts, and if my plan doesn't work, cut off my nose."

CHAPTER FIFTEEN

The Bagha Singh Family

According to Abul Fazal, author of the famous *Ain-E-Akbari*, the Khandayat caste used to be the real landlords of Orissa, holding all the important royal positions, from soldier to custodian of records, in the durbar of the Gajapati kings. They did not receive cash from the royal treasury for their services. Instead, they were given land, so that, from one generation to the other, most land in Orissa became theirs as hereditary holdings. Orissa remained independent for a long time only because of their power: for more than three long years the Pathans, who ruled Bengal, tried to invade Orissa, but they failed to cross even the Subaranarekha River. The Khandayat soldiers did not have to spend all their time in the durbar: the commanders lived with their soldiers in nearby villages, each forming a group called a chakra. Attached to the commander's house was a choupadhi, where the four martial arts—wrestling, fencing, archery, and shooting—were taught. After the fall of the Gajapati kings, Todarmal settled the bigger choupadhis under the title of killas. Even today in many places in

Orissa, there are small choupadhis, where the descendants of the once mighty commanders still live.

Our Bagha Singh family was descended from one such ancient commander. Their real surname was Malla, and the eldest son held the title Bagha Singh. It was the Bagha Singh who inherited the hereditary holdings, and his brothers were entitled to an annuity called bhatia. The present Bagha Singh family was no longer wealthy; yet, just as a deodar tree looks tall in a treeless field, they seemed important and were treated as such in the area. The choupadhi in the village of Ratanpur was a rent-free holding for Khandayats. Besides this, there was the zamindari of Fatepur Sarsandha, and some other lesser zamindaris. Natabar Ghanasyam Bagha Singh had squandered all his property: generous to a fault, he spared no thought for the future as he opened his purse. He gave and spent recklessly; no one ever heard him say no to someone asking him for money. Beggars and wandering singers never left his door empty-handed; no one ever felt ashamed to come to his house bowl in hand, begging for food. He was a lover of good food, and took great delight in feeding others. Villagers said the flat rice pancakes, the cakes stuffed with sweet shredded coconut, and the puddings made from palua flour, with which Bagha Singh lovingly entertained his guests, were simply unforgettable.

Natabar Ghanasyam Bagha Singh had borrowed vast sums of money during his lifetime. Soon after he died, all the zamindaris, except the Khandayati one, had to be sold off. He had four sons: the eldest was called Bhimsen Bagha Singh and his brothers were Prahlad Malla, Kutuli Malla, and Balaram Malla. The sons were not extravagant like their father; they conducted their affairs with great prudence. Although they were no longer as wealthy as they used to be, they managed to carry on somehow. Even when tattered, good silk cloth remains silk: people continued to respect the Bagha Singhs because of their glorious past. Apart from them, there were eighteen families of milkmen, barbers, and sweetmeat makers in the village of Ratanpur. Whenever the Bagha Singhs needed their services, the villagers worked without asking for payment. A priest lived in the village, and there were eight Dom families as well: they had been given free landholdings for playing the drums on festive occasions.

A bitter dispute had been going on between the Bagha Singh family and Mangaraj for three years now. Although Mangaraj was very clever and without a match in the law courts, the mere sight of a lathi would make him run away. As for the Bagha Singhs, they thought all problems in the world could be solved with lathis.

Mangaraj's men dared not enter Ratanpur for fear of the Doms. But the Doms were now in jail; stolen goods had been found buried in their backyards. Everyone said that no Dom was ever a thief, but Mangaraj had spent two bags of money, and they had been convicted.

The other day, Balaram Malla gave Mangaraj a mouthful, from the verandah of the shop in Gobindapur, because Mangaraj's cows had ruined the crops in a number of fields in Ratanpur. Mangaraj had not dared utter a word in reply. Ratanpur was four miles from Gobindapur, but since its rice fields lay close to Gobindapur, Mangaraj's cows would stray into them and often destroy the crops.

CHAPTER SIXTEEN

The Auntie from Tangi

It was Snana Purnima, a hot and humid day in the month of Jyestha. On the day of Snana Purnima, Lord Jagannath retires to his sick room. For over two months now, not one solitary drop of rain had fallen from the skies. The air was still. Trees bare of leaves stood stiff like the Garuda Pillar in front of Lord Jagannath. Not even the leaves on the aswatha tree stirred. The sand on the village path was so hot, a handful of grains thrown on it instantly turned into puffed rice. The stray bitch of the village rolled in the mud by the edge of the pond, sticking out its tongue, as it lay gasping, but not venturing into the water. Perhaps the water was boiling. Not a single cow or calf grazed in the fields; they lay beneath the trees, chewing their cuds, looking like baishnavas, moving their mouths as if they were repeating the divine name, their eyes closed, counting their beads. Not a single crow flew across the sky. The birds took shelter among the leaves and gasped for breath. The sun was so hot it could crack one's skull. It was already well past noon, yet the sky continued to rain embers.

Hum, my brother, hum hum
Watch brother, hum hum
Work harder, turn right, hum hum
Turn left, hum, hum.

These words chanted by palanquin bearers carried across the road to the village of Ratanpur. Attendants with five loads of gifts walked behind the palanquin, which was completely covered with a thick cloth. At this time of day, there were no menfolk in the village. Since the cultivation season had not yet begun, they had all gone with the Bagha Singh brothers to the Snana festival of Lord Baladev in Kendrapada.

There was great commotion in the village; news of the arrival of the palanquin quickly spread from one end to the other. Old and middle-aged women opened their doors and stepped out into the village path; young women peeped out, showing only their nose rings. A great debate, concerning the occupant of the palanquin, began: first, they argued about the gender, then about the status of the occupant. Some said the palanquin carried a newly married girl; others thought the occupant was the police inspector; and for still others, it contained a Sahib. Jema's mother produced some irrefutable arguments in favor of her belief that the occupant must be none other than the police inspector taking loads of vegetables home on Snana Purnima. Had the palanquin not moved in the direction of the Bagha Singh house, there was a strong possibility her contention would have gained the status of established truth. The bearers set the palanquin down in front of the Bagha Singh house and fanned themselves with their towels, for they were sweating profusely; with their left hand, they wiped handfuls of sweat off their faces. Word was sent into the house that the aunt of the youngest daughter-in-law had arrived. Bagha Singh's son, Chandramni, had married the daughter of Fateh Singh of Dalijoda in the month of Makara. The sharp-witted village women needed no further evidence to reach the conclusion that the palanquin had come straight from Dalijoda. Manika, the barber woman, hurried to inform the ladies of the house.

You must have heard of Manika. If not, then you must. She was no mere barber woman; she was any man's match in cleverness and in her capacity for intrigue. People in the village were scared of her. Even old and middle-aged woman sought her advice on matters of importance. She was unrivaled in her various skills. If a newborn baby fell sick, she could cure it through her spells. She was an excellent midwife, too; she took care of a woman from the beginning of her confinement until she was delivered of the baby. Her knowledge of herbs and roots was extensive. She was as eager to pick a quarrel as she was keen to do a good turn: when she got involved in a fight she could completely forget even to take her daily bath; but, if you had once had a few good words for her, the same Manika would sit by your sick bed and tenderly nurse you back to health. On festive days or weddings, she would arrive of her own volition, and do all the work, whether or not you invited her. There was nothing she could not do. It was from her that the village women learned everything about the world outside: the goings-on in Cuttack, the deeds of the Sahibs, the stories about the Jagannath temple in Puri, and so on.

There may be ponds without fish, but there cannot be villages without maligners. Some said Manika was a chatterbox, a liar, an impudent woman. Three generations of her ancestors had never gone beyond the boundaries of the village, how could she know so many things about Cuttack and the Sahibs? But Manika was very well thought of in the Bagha Singh household: the ladies of the household sent for her every evening to listen to her often-told stories of the adventures of four friends in foreign lands—a prince, a minister's son, a merchant's son, and the son of a royal guard. They also liked her to tell the story of the girl called Kalarei Dei, and the one about the goddess whose abode was on the other side of the river. Manika could narrate nonstop the story of the battle between Lord Rama and the demon Ravana. She had answers to all your questions. But you had to say yes to whatever she said. If you failed to do so, there would be no end to your troubles. Anyway, a woman who was so well known must be lucky. Manika was so famous in the village that it is not at all necessary for us to introduce her to our readers.

As the palanquin was being borne along the village path, Manika talked to the barber walking behind it, and found out who its occupant was. She ran into the Bagha Singh house shouting, "Oh, my Saantanis, where are you all? Come out quickly! Our new daughter-in-law's aunt has arrived from Dalijoda. Her palanquin has been outside for quite some time. I heard about her plan to visit us four days ago, but alas, I forgot all about it. She actually started out yesterday from Dalijoda. I was wondering why she was so late arriving here. On the way she stopped near the big pond for a wash; so she was delayed." All four daughters-in-law in the Bagha Singh household looked at each other in utter confusion. They were at a loss as to how to treat this uninvited aunt, but Manika at once came to their rescue. "Go and bring our aunt into the house," she instructed.

Two or three jewel-studded noses now became visible through

the half-opened front door. The aunt stepped out of the palanquin and strode inside. "My dear sisters, my dear sisters," she exclaimed, folding the women in her embrace. The ladies of the house took her by the hand and cordially led her into the inner precincts. Manika's eagerness and anxiety to extend proper hospitality exceeded everyone else's; she ran ahead, and with great promptness, spread out a four-arm-lengths-long carpet in front of Bagha Singh's bedroom. The aunt sat down on it, drew the ladies near, and sat them down beside her. Five loads of gifts were brought in and placed in the middle of the courtyard: one load contained ripe mangoes, the second, large ripe jack-fruits, the third, ripe and green bananas, in the fourth and fifth loads were four large earthen pots, the mouths covered with banana leaves washed with rice paste. That was all. The village women rushed in to see the gifts—Rebati, Sukuri, Sakri, Malia, Jema's mother, Bhima's mother and aunt, Hagura's mother, Sadari, Menki, Kanaka, Netajeji, Sabi, Kamali, Padiapa, Shyama's daughter-in-law, Nalita, Bishakha, and Sumitra, the young daughter-in-law of the cowman's family. Some women came carrying their babies, some arrived with their children in tow, others came in small groups, and some on their own. Sukra's mother had been in the middle of spreading cow dung on her earthen floor; she came running without stopping to wash her hands, which she kept raised like a snake's hood. Bagha Singh's courtyard was packed with this throng of women, who stared at the newly arrived aunt like devotees meditating on the face of the image of a goddess. But the naughty boys of the village—Bankia, Kalia, Banamalia, Gopalia, Ramia, Umeshia, Kashia, Daitaria, and others—were not interested in the guest's physical appearance; they looked greedily at the ripe bananas and mangoes stored nearby, just as a cat eyes a basket of salted fish. There could be no doubt that they were violating all the norms of civilized conduct. As the circle of boys began closing in around the fruit, clever Manika sensed their evil intentions and drove them away with a quick gesture of her right hand. In doing so, she prevented an unlawful incident of looting from taking place.

Our "aunt" wore a vermilion mark on her forehead, as large as the one on the image of Goddess Budhi Mangala. She had put on kajal, and from her nose hung an ornament set with the image of a dancing peacock. A jewel glittered on the left side of her nose, and she wore two huge earrings. A large heavy necklace adorned her neck, alongside a silken string beaded with gold coins. She wore armlets, metal bangles, and bracelets, too. On her five fingers, there were seven silver rings inscribed with names. Her feet were decorated with two heavy brass anklets, and there were rings on all her toes. Her hair was tied into a huge top-knot, ornamented with all kinds of pins. She was dressed in a very expensive Berhampuri sari and was chewing a mouthful of betel leaves with great relish. Everyone had heard that the Fateh Singh family of Dalijoda was wealthy, and now, seeing all the ornaments worn by the aunt from Dalijoda, they had the chance to see how rich the family really was.

As soon as she had sat down, the aunt asked, "Where is my niece? Where is she? I want to see her. Ah, my motherless little girl must have grown weak." One of the Saatanis brought in the new daughter-in-law, her face completely covered with the end of her sari. She approached slowly, lowering her head, and fell at the feet of the aunt to pay her respects. The aunt clasped her to her bosom and started to wail, "Oh, my dear daughter, my eyes went blind pining to see you. Oh, light of our house, our house become dark after you left us. Oh, priceless jewel."

So she went on, until fully exhausted. Profuse tears ceaselessly flowed from her eyes. A lady of the house took the guest into her arms, wiped away her tears, consoled and comforted her. The aunt said, "What can I say, dear sister. Ever since my niece left me, even food tastes bitter, and I feel no joy in anything. I keep watching the road all day long, and whenever I see a traveler, I ask him if my daughter is coming to visit us."

The niece was dumbfounded by the sound of this unfamiliar voice and by the loud wailing. Driven by curiosity she tried to glimpse the aunt's face, lifting the end of her sari. But the shrewd aunt could sense what the young daughter-in-law was up to and, pulling back the end of the sari, covered the daughter-in-law's face, saying, "Oh, my shy one, I know no one surpasses your modesty. No one need tell you how to behave in front of your elders. My sister, your mother, was so shy that all her life she never even raised her eyes to see the face of her mother-in-law and other in-laws. She would shout abuse at them with her face respectfully covered. Like mother, like daughter. Shame on a young woman who forgets propriety and becomes forward. Of course, my niece need not be told all this."

On hearing the sermon, the daughter-in-law gathered her clothes more tightly around herself and squatted like a frog. She had heard that her mother's cousin lived in Tangi, and so she thought the visitor must be this aunt.

After this, the aunt had a long and lively talk with the ladies of the house. They exchanged many pleasantries. You would perhaps like to hear what they talked about, but we do not intend to report the small talk of women from a respectable family. However, if you are really curious, we can tell you a few harmless things. The aunt said, "Everything has gone well for us this year. Everyone in our village has left for the festival of Lord Baladev, and it seemed a good opportunity for me too: I could go and see Lord Baladev, as well as visit you, my sister. Also, I could find out how my dear niece is doing. So I forced everyone in our family to set out on this journey: my husband and brother-in-law have gone on ahead on horseback and are waiting for me in the grove nearby. The barbers and the bearers are with them. I insisted that I would not proceed without seeing my niece, and then I set out on my own. Tomorrow all of us will return here after seeing Lord Baladev. On my way, I heard that your husband—my dear brother-in-law—has also gone to the festival. Excellent, all of us will come back together. It is a pity, my dear sisters, that we cannot talk to our hearts' content today. But I promise that on my way back I will stay for at least four days. My sister's husband said that we should stop for only one day, but, mark my words, they will spend no fewer than four. I will make them stay, by hook or by crook."

After this announcement, she stroked her niece's head and said, "Oh, my poor little daughter. It is a long time since you last saw me. You were so small then, that you may not even recognize me now. But let me come back. We will talk for a long time, all by ourselves." And she whispered into her ear, "I will bring you lots of good things from the festival."

The aunt stood up, saying that she wanted to go out to make water. "Sister, when I go out to the fields to answer the call of nature, I always take a bath. If I go out four times in one day I take four baths. But if I go out only to make water, then one jug of water is enough. One has to be very scrupulous in performing one's ablutions."

So saying, she hurried to the palanquin and took a jug from one of the bearers, who had kept the mouth of the jug carefully covered with his hands. The aunt then went out into the backyard, and one of Bagha Singh's maidservants, Muturi's mother, showed her the way. The aunt turned to her and said, "I have not made water since morning and I feel terribly uncomfortable. But, I cannot do it if anyone, even a woman, is looking at me."

Muturi's mother bowed and said, "Very well, very well. There is no one around. Don't worry. I will leave." And she came away, closing the door to the backyard.

It was already getting dark. The aunt rose and said, "I cannot stay any longer. They are all waiting for me." Her hostesses wanted her to eat something, but our aunt bit her tongue, exclaiming, "Oh, Ram, oh, Ram! How could you suggest such a thing, sisters, how could you? Have I not given my daughter in marriage to this house? How can I touch food here?"

As she took her leave, the aunt embraced the Bagha Singh women and sang,

Farewell my sister, my heart with you I am leaving
All night and all day I will be thinking of you, and weeping.

The palanquin left the village by the road cutting across the rice fields, and soon disappeared into the darkness of the night. The loads of gifts left behind were now gathered in one place to be shown to the Bagha Singh brothers when they returned.

After the aunt had left, her person and her character became the subject of a long and lively discussion. All praised her: some praised her beauty, some her character; some admired her ornaments, and some the ripe bananas she had brought. But Manika remarked, "True, she comes from a fine family, but she is not at all good-looking. Two of her front teeth stick out, and she has very ungainly cheeks."

Hagura's mother joined in, "Her voice was not at all sweet, it grates on the ear."

"She stomps rather than walks," added Muturi's mother.

And Sankhi agreed with her, "Very true. And her laugh was awful."

In the opinion of Sukuri, the aunt had ugly, staring eyes. In no time, all her good qualities were, in this manner, disputed and discounted. When the young daughter-in-law was asked about the visitor, all she replied was, "She must be the auntie from Tangi."

CHAPTER SEVENTEEN

House on Fire

Today a great calamity has befallen the village of Ratanpur; there is wailing and weeping everywhere. A great fire which started at midnight last night has swept through the Bagha Singh house, destroying everything, including the granary. Only the walls, charred and covered with ash, remain standing. The fire has not yet died out. The thatched roofs have collapsed in flames, and the bamboo center beams are crackling in the intense heat. The pillars resemble columns of fire. On some of the walls, pieces of bamboo and bunches of straw are still ablaze, and the doors are ablaze, the doorframes too. There is fire everywhere. The flames have reached the granary; large clouds of smoke are pouring out of it. It is high summer, the month of Jyestha, and the thatch and beams were tinder-dry. When they caught fire, who would have dared go near the house? A wind rose and the fire spread everywhere, except for the roof. The farmhands are busy throwing pitchers of water onto the flames, trying to fight their way into the room with the atoo roof. The villagers who had gone off to the Snana festival have all come back.

It was now midday. The sky above was ablaze, and, below, the house was on fire. Not even a piece of straw could be saved. The house had caught fire at midnight. The women of the house, who were fast sleep, had awoken with a start. Howling in fear and confusion, they had run out in whatever clothes they had on and were now sitting helplessly under a tree, looking at the house on fire and wailing like frightened wild animals. The farmhands untethered the cattle and kept away from the fire. Had they tried harder, they could perhaps have saved many more things. But who would risk his own life to save other people's property? The day wore on. No one in the Bagha Singh family had so much as cleaned his teeth since daybreak. The children and the women were feeling faint, for they had not eaten anything. The old family priest, Kelu Ratha, came and comforted them, got them to wash their faces and clean their teeth, and brought them some rice flakes and rice water. Some ate, some did not. Bagha Singh drank a jug of water and sank to the ground. Except for the granary, the fire had now died down. Wisps of smoke still drifted out from a few rooms.

Night came. Bagha Singh, his brothers, and a few villagers were all sitting under a tree. Bagha Singh asked, "How did the house catch fire?"

Everyone else asked the same question, but who had the answer?

Kelu Ratha wondered, "Who would dare set fire to the Bagha Singh house? It must be the work of Goddess Hingula herself." All kept staring at him, feeling he was right.

But Gobinda Ratha said, "No, no, that's not true. Goddess

Budhi Mangala's anger brought this about. Mangaraj offers her puja all year round. Several times I urged you to send her offerings, but you never listened to me. Now, see what has happened. You know that I am not given to saying anything without a great deal of thought. If it wasn't the work of a goddess, how can you explain that the fire started in the hayrick in the backyard?"

Manika said, "Whatever the case may be, our new daughter-in-law has brought us bad luck. Since she came to this house we've had a series of bad things happen around here."

"I agree with you," Shyama's mother remarked. "Until now, I had kept my mouth shut because I was afraid. Don't you remember how a snake bit Bagha Singh's cow in the month of Chaitra. Were there no snakes in the village before? Did they ever bite cows? I am forty-eight years old and I don't remember a snake ever biting a cow."

Makara, a farmhand, joined in. "You're right. Two years ago, my bullocks, which were big and strong like elephants, suddenly collapsed."

"Our cows used to graze in this field in large numbers," Arjun, another farmhand added. "But this year, not a single one is to be seen."

After long arguments, and much guesswork, the farmhands, the barber women, and the housemaids reached the incontrovertible conclusion that the new daughter-in-law's arrival was the cause of the fire. Manika put forward, in support of this, "See, not even three days have passed since our new daughter-in-law's aunt was here. And now this disaster."

Bagha Singh enquired, "What aunt? Who was here?"

Manika promptly began narrating how the aunt had come

from Dalijoda, riding in a palanquin, how Fateh Singh of Dalijoda had gone ahead on horseback to see Lord Baladev. She also told him about the five loads of gifts the aunt had brought with her. She spiced up her narrative with a little help from her imagination. Sabi's mother, the fishwife, said, "I have often visited Gobindapur in the past to sell rice flakes, and to me, the aunt from Dalijoda looked a lot like Champa, the maidservant in Mangaraj's house."

And Shankar, the farmhand, added, "The man carrying the load of jack-fruit was one of Mangaraj's own farmhands."

The Bagha Singh brothers looked at each other. "We returned directly from Kendrapada," they said, "but we did not meet any palanquin or horse on our way."

That same night, messengers were sent out to Fateh Singh of Dalijoda, and to Kendrapada as well. They returned, saying that the whole affair was a hoax; no aunt of the new daughter-in-law lived in Dalijoda. For many days, people in the village discussed the incident. People in the neighboring villages also talked about it. All said that it was surely the work of Goddess Budhi Mangala. But we believe that it was the work of a wily and wicked witch.

Fateh Singh of Dalijoda came and took his daughter home. People say the girl was so distraught, she had given up food and water; she would have died if her father had not come to take her away.

CHAPTER EIGHTEEN

Saantani

All shall pass away when their time comes;
but their deeds shall be remembered for ever.

It was the auspicious day of Radhastami, in the month of Shra-bana. The time was early morning, and it was fairly dark. Every-one was still in bed, although a few people were already awake. Unless there was urgent work to be done, most people did not feel like leaving their beds so early, during the winter and rainy months. Marua, Mangaraj's maidservant, came out, carrying a jug in her left hand, opening the door with the other. When she stepped out, her eyes fell on the rectangular platform where a tulsi, the sacred basil plant, grew. She stopped dead. What was that white object lying there? The platform was in front of Saan-tani's room, in the middle of the second courtyard of Mangaraj's house. All her life, Saantani had been intensely devoted to the worship of Goddess Brindabati, who is embodied in this plant. She had, herself, brought a sapling from the grove, and had it planted on the platform. Most of her day was spent cleaning it, purifying it with water mixed with cow dung, watering it, offering fine rice to Goddess Brindabati, and lighting wicks. She had very little time left for anything else.

Marua approached the platform cautiously and took a careful look. What was this! It was Saantani herself! "Oh, Saantani, oh, Saantani," she called. There was no answer. Marua put down the jug and shook the sleeping figure. There had been a heavy downpour during the night, and Saantani's clothes were wet and muddied, her body as stiff as wood and as cold as hailstones. Marua shrieked and began wailing, "Oh, my dear Saantani, oh, my dear Saantani, why have you left us? Why? Who will care for a poor creature like me now? Who will cook an invalid's diet for me when I am sick? Oh, my dear Saantani!" Hearing Marua's loud wailing, everyone in the house came running out. Soon the courtyard was full. Everybody wept. The daughters-in-law forgot to cover their faces; weeping bitterly, they sank to the ground. But Champa surpassed everyone in her loud lamentation. She ran the length of the house, from the front door to the back, howling. Who could console whom when everyone was weeping? The news of Saantani's death spread with the speed of lightning. Women left their daily chores, and men abandoned their work. All began reciting the sterling qualities of the departed soul. Even women who were not related to Saantani could not hold back their tears. Some remarked, "With her death on this auspicious day of Radhastami, Goddess Lakshmi has forsaken the village for ever." Others added, "Mangaraj's days of prosperity are now over; from now on, his fortunes will decline."

Whenever the subject of devotion to one's husband came up in the village, everyone would mention Saantani's loyalty to

Mangaraj. Her character was noble, and she was pious by nature. Fate had denied her a husband's affection, which is what a woman treasures most, but she suffered the neglect without complaint. She simply believed that to serve her husband was her sacred duty, and performing this duty gave her joy. She found great happiness in that, and indeed, in serving all mankind. Her sons, ever since they had come of age, did not take care of her. The daughters-in-law did not disrespect her, but they did not show her the respect due the head of the family. No one had ever seen them massage her limbs when she took ill. In a way, this behavior of theirs was due to Saantani's own actions. It was not in her nature to assert herself; she treated everyone equally and did not have it in her to exercise control over anyone; perhaps she had no desire to dominate. She liked those who obeyed her and also those who did not.

If anyone said anything harsh to her she remained quiet. Just as it is difficult to know whether a salagram stone is in a sitting or a sleeping position, no one could tell whether she was happy or unhappy. She never entered into quarrels with anyone, she never discussed anything with anyone, she hardly ever talked. When someone in the house fell ill, she would go and sit by the patient day and night, lovingly massaging their limbs; it did not matter to her whether the patient was her own daughter-in-law or a mere maidservant. If she knew that someone in the house or outside had gone without food, she would not touch even water until she had fed that person with her own hands. She always took care of the poor, the old, orphans, and widows. If she learned that someone had no food at home, she should secretly send them a measure of rice, some lentils, a little salt, oil, a slice of pumpkin, a few lady fingers, and so on. When a woman in the village was about to give birth, Saantani would send her own maidservants to look after her. The poor and luckless were always confident she would come to their help. It is said that many debtors and poor tenants escaped Mangaraj's wrath thanks to her kindness: if someone was being harassed by Mangaraj, he would get relief by sending his daughter or daughter-in-law to Saantani for help. She would suffer Mangaraj's anger and abuse because she had come to their rescue. On such occasions, Champa would make barbed comments, which she bore in silence, as if deaf to Champa's words. Saantani found great joy in doing good. As Pandit Sibu put it, in his pure and exalted diction, Saantani was the living embodiment of such heavenly qualities as kindness, love, and devotion.

There was, however, one peculiar trait in Saantani's character. We cannot decide whether it was a flaw or a virtue. We leave that up to you. She did not know how to color and embroider her speech by making up all kinds of things. Not only that, she spoke so softly that no one walking past her house could ever overhear her. But if Mangaraj lost his temper with a servant or a housemaid, and raised his hand to mete out a beating, Saantani would come forward and defend them with a series of arguments proving their innocence. On occasions like these, Saantani would think nothing of the difference between truth and falsehood; she could tell a lie in order to help the servants. It was she who would then bear the brunt of Mangaraj's wrath. True, to tell a lie to save the culprit, and to take punishment for the crimes committed by others, is not how an intelligent person acts and behaves. But Saantani never changed her ways. It is said that a person's deeper nature is constant. She wept at the suffering of people, no matter whether they were guilty or not.

Another thing, whenever a quarrel broke out between two

maidservants or between two daughters-in-law, it was observed that Saantani always took the side of the weak. This showed that she was not an impartial person at all. She did not seem to feel one should give support only after due deliberation.

Saantani had one serious shortcoming, and we have to call it "serious" since her husband was always vexed with her for it: she was not in the least worldly-wise; she had no idea that money was such a precious thing. She never sought it, so she never had any. If she ever came by a coin or two—worth only a rupee or maybe four annas—she would put them away in a pot where grain was stored, or keep them on a beam in the thatched eaves. This money she would give to Mukunda to buy a sari or a gift for a girl in the village at the time of her marriage, or she would send it to someone in need. In the absence of eyewitnesses, we have gathered this information from hearsay.

Anyway, it does not matter whether Saantani was a good or a bad person; when she died, everyone shed tears, everyone except one. Struck dumb, unable to open his toothless mouth, his long bony legs outstretched, Mukunda, an old farmhand, sat against a hedge and stared blankly into space. It was he who did not cry. Are you interested in knowing his age, caste, lineage, and birthplace? Probably not, for who cares about a poor farmhand, who was also an orphan? He himself said that he had been sent out to call the midwife when Saantani was born. He used to carry her in his arms when she was a little girl. And when she married, he accompanied her to her in-law's house. One good soul recognizes another—only Mukunda knew what Saantani felt. Whenever Saantani was unhappy for some reason, Mukunda would come near her and, with sorrow and sympathy in his eyes, look at her steadily. Then, Saantani would lower her eyes. Everything was said in that silent exchange, and Saantani would feel comforted. Mukunda, whose eyes would fill with tears at Saantani's slightest suffering, had no tears in his eyes today. A man does not cry when everything—his joy, his peace, his support, his hope, his comfort—has been destroyed. Now and then he heaved a deep sigh, and that was the only sign that he was alive.

Sitting near Saantani's body, Mangaraj gazed listlessly at her face. Tears rolled down his cheeks. No one had ever seen Mangaraj shed tears; this was the first time people saw him cry. They believed he was incapable of love, affection, shame, and decency; they believed that for him money was everything, that day and night, he thought about nothing else. He was often seen sitting silently with a strange glint in his eyes. Dreams of wealth rose and disappeared before his eyes, like waves of the sea rushing to the shore, crashing and dissolving. But today his mind was filled with something else. His eyes were half-closed, listless, and moist with tears. Maybe he was crying for Saantani. No man can endure the loss of a dear one. Had Mangaraj ever understood the heavenly sweetness and beauty of conjugal love? Had anyone ever heard him utter even a word of affection to Saantani? Why, then, should he grieve for her today? Nonetheless, we trust that he was now suffering the pangs of separation. No matter whether a wife is good or bad, one cannot help developing some attachment to her. No human being can remain untouched by this heavenly sentiment, when a marriage has been solemnized in front of the sacred fire and eight holy pitchers. A wife is your partner in everything: she is the begetter of your beloved children, she shares your sorrows and your joys, she comforts you when you are sick, she is your friend in need. Even if you are a stone-hearted man and are unable to understand her qualities or have not loved her when she was alive, you will nevertheless suffer the agony of separation at her death. There are no words to describe this pain, especially if one has had the good fortune of living with a chaste and devoted wife. This can be felt only in the heart. A man bitten by a cobra can only suffer the pain, he cannot communicate it in words. He alone knows how the venom spreads and tears through the veins, and how the heart dries up. For him the beauty of all beautiful things, the sweetness of all sweet things, the fragrance of all flowers, and the melody of all music—all the things of value in life—no longer exist. In short, he feels like a dead man among the living, and a living being among the dead.

Two separate streams flowed through Mangaraj's life: one was turbulent, infested with snakes and crocodiles, and like the Charmaswati, it kept overflowing its banks; but the other, full of pure sweet water, flowed underground, like the River Falgu. Perhaps Mangaraj realized that the River Falgu in his life had now dried up for ever. If a bowl of wine and a bowl of water are placed in front of a drunkard, he will certainly prefer the former; only when he is desperately thirsty does he realize that though wine is intoxicating, water gives life.

Having observed Mangaraj, we conclude that he was overcome with sorrow, as well as repentance. A man weeps when he is stricken with grief, but repentance does not bring tears to his eyes. Grief is like burning embers, but repentance is like a cold, consuming fire. Did he now repent because he sensed a connection between his misdeeds, his neglect of Saantani, and her death? He had committed innumerable crimes, but no one had ever seen him contrite. How could one be sure? How could one be certain about human nature, which changes from moment to moment? The creator has fashioned all men and women from the same elements. Just as blood, flesh, bone, and feces make up a body, so too elements such as kindness, attachment, love, affection, jealousy, hostility, and cruelty form the mind. A man is fully a man only when all these elements are in proper harmony, but he loses his humanity when one element comes to dominate. When that happens man turns into either a god or a demon. In other words, man is both heavenly and satanic. Would you not call someone a god if you learned that he had sacrificed his own life to save someone else's? But, if you learned that someone had murdered a child for a few pieces of gold, would you not take him for a cruel demon such as those in mythology? But such extreme examples are very rare: human beings always remain human. Although all human beings are created from the same elements, their outward behavior differs. In physical appearance, no two human beings are completely alike. So too does their nature also differ. Some, for instance, are strong-minded, some are weak, and some have dormant minds. At times, under the pressure of a strange combination of events, the faculties of their mind come to life. Who could have foreseen that Jagai and Madhai, who were drunkards and lechers, would become great devotees of Lord Krishna? Saul, who was an enemy of the Christians and cruelly persecuted them, was later transformed into Saint Paul. On the contrary, all the merit earned by the great rishi Viswamitra, through harsh austerities endured over thousands of years, was destroyed by a single amorous glance from Menaka, the dancer.

Consider carefully these sudden changes in human character, their root cause, and their meaning. Here, we recall the saying of the great sage Sankaracharya,

Kṣaṇam iha sajjanasaṃgatir ekā
bhavati bhāvārṇabataraṇī naukā

We can safely sail on the ocean of life,
*If we are blessed with the company of a good soul, even for a moment.**

The Brahmos also teach, "Condemn the sin, not the sinner."

How can we tell whether the emotion that inspires remorse in men was not now awakened in Mangaraj's heart? We are not omniscient and cannot see into other people's hearts. How can we fathom Mangaraj's? Even if we could, we would not find words to describe how grief and repentance together had rendered him insensible to the world outside. We have said many things, just as a dumb person desperately tries to say something by throwing about his hands and legs.

Dear reader, please permit us to stop here. The drummers have begun beating their drums to mark the start of the funeral procession. Sadhaba women have already lined the village path to throw flowers and cowries on the litter carrying Saantani's mortal remains. We should be silent now.

Haribol, Haribol! In the name of the Lord. In the name of the Lord!

---

*An accurate translation, and quite possibly a view that is close to Senapati's own.

CHAPTER NINETEEN

The Police Inquiry

Night gave way to day in Gobindapur as always, but the sun was not yet visible. There were clouds in the sky, and it was drizzling. It is said that morning clouds are no clouds, because they do not bring rain; likewise, guests who arrive in the morning are no guests, since they leave before sunset. The sky had now cleared somewhat. The rice fields had already been weeded, and the farmers had no need to go there at this time of year. Someone was grinding something on his outer verandah; someone else was busy cleaning the cowshed; another person was going out to cut some grass for the cows, smoking a homemade pipe, a palm-leaf hat on his head, a length of bamboo on his shoulders, a piece of string and a sickle in his hands; yet another had climbed onto his thatched roof and was arranging the pumpkin creepers. Learning that there was no salt in the house, Hari Puhan was trying to prove by all sorts of arguments that his wife was a spendthrift. Having finished their morning chores the women were on their way to the fields. *Jhas dhum, Jhas dhum,* the weavers' quarter had started resounding with the sound of shuttles flying back and forth. The spindles rattled as the weaver women worked them on their verandahs.

It was early in the morning. Sama Sahu's farmhand, Gopal Samal, his head protected by a palm-leaf hat, was busy repairing a ditch in a rice field. Ghusuria, one of Mangaraj's farmhands, ran along a neighboring field toward Gobara Jena's house. When he saw Gopalia, he beckoned to him to come near: "I am going on a very secret errand. It's something important. I trust you, that's why I'm telling you." Then he whispered something in Gopalia's ear. "Be careful. No one else should know. That's master's order."

On his way, Ghusuria ran into a Pana. Again, he whispered something in his ear, telling him to keep the matter a secret, and moved on. Then he came upon Danei Sahu, Binodia, Natharia, and Bhima's mother; they were all taken into his confidence and told to keep the matter to themselves. Meanwhile, Gopalia stopped working and rushed to tell Sama Sahu, his master. Sama Sahu told Hari Sahu, Hatia told Natia, Jemama told Shyama's mother, and mother-in-law passed the news on to daughter-in-law. So the story went round the village. Everyone spoke in whispers, and everyone was told to keep the story a secret. Some said the jamadar was about to arrive. Someone protested, "No, it is a murder case. The daroga himself will come on horseback." But knowledgeable people remarked gravely, "Do you think this matter involves ordinary people like us? A company paltoon will be sent from Cuttack. No doubt a lot of people from the village will be arrested. That is bound to happen." After that, the whole village became extremely quiet. After a quick dip in the pond, the women ran off in their wet clothes; the clothes dripped and flapped around them as they hurried home. Their panic was such that they could not even fill their pitchers to the brim; the half-filled pitchers made loud slapping noises, like the tongues of native patriots haranguing a gathering. Clutching his cane, the village schoolmaster disappeared. Children scattered on the path. Like a policeman dragging an accused murderer, the headboy marched a small boy to the school. Now this same boy was running away faster than everyone else.

Ghusuria came back and informed Mangaraj that Gobara Jena was not at home; in fact, he had not returned home last night. Mangaraj then sent a farmhand to the weavers' quarter. Afterward, he himself went there; but, moving from house to house he ran into no one. The doors of all the houses were locked; there was no one to be seen. Back home, he walked about restlessly, extremely worried. Unable to find anyone, he did not know what to do. Ghusuria, wielding a stick, chased a stray dog out of the backyard. A pair of jackals stood staring out of a kia bush.

It was now well past midday. A large man riding a small horse was seen approaching from the east. The rider's beard covered his chest, and he wore a chapkan, a cap, and a pair of loose pajamas. The horse came trotting along gaily. Five chowkidars with lathis on their shoulders ran breathlessly in front and behind. At the head of the procession was Gobara Jena, carrying his lathi. The rider got off his horse, saying, "Bismillah," and released a deep sigh of relief.

A little later, another man was seen riding along the village path. His horse was skinny; its ribs stuck out. Its hind legs were now hairless and covered with sores from rubbing against each other; its eyes bulged out of their sockets. On its back was a seat of thick red cloth. The rider was large and heavy; his clothes were those of a rich person: a Maniabandhi dhoti, an embroidered shirt, and a silk pugree on his head. A chowkidar carrying a lathi on his left shoulder walked behind the horse. He kept prodding it along with a stick, clucking his tongue. The attendant, a Pana boy, dragged the horse forward, pulling at its rein. Stretching its neck the poor horse tottered along. Like his predecessor, this rider too got off in front of Mangaraj's house. However, while dismounting, his weight supported by two men, he fell flat on his face. He got up immediately and delivered a resounding slap to one of them to indicate that he had fallen because of their carelessness. How, otherwise, could such an expert horseman have taken a fall? As for the horse, as soon as its rider dismounted and before the attendant could even blink, it collapsed and rolled on the ground three or four times like a devotee rolling in the dust before the chariot of Lord Jagannath. Then it picked itself up. Meanwhile, its rider gingerly sought out the places on his body where he had scabs and began to scratch himself vigorously.

Sheikh Inayat Husain was a top-class daroga of Cuttack district. He had an excellent command of Persian. In his view, Oriya was the language of simpletons; therefore, he never wrote in Oriya, and he signed government papers only in Persian. In recognition of his competence, he had been in charge of the Kendrapada police station for the last twelve years. There had been a rumor last year that he would be transferred elsewhere, but this was only because he had failed to send the usual gifts for the peshkar and sirastadar in the headquarters at Cuttack on time. His companion, Munshi Chakradhar Das, was a very experienced police clerk. Chowkidars could tell you that the magistrate Sahib was always very pleased with the reports the munshi wrote.

The police party sat in front of Mangaraj's kacheri. Daroga Sheikh Inayat Husain was seated on a mat, his beard covering his chest. In front of him, on his right, sat Munshi Chakradhar Das;

the cloth seat that earlier had been on the back of his horse was now spread out on a grass mat. At a distance of twenty arm-lengths and facing them, stood Police Constables Golam Kadar and Hari Singh, as well as five chowkidars. They kept a strict watch over Mangaraj, who was now under arrest. He sat there, his head hanging low. A large crowd had gathered near Mangaraj's house. There was a strict order that no one should enter the house and no one leave it. The women of the house were made to stand aside while the house was thoroughly searched: chests and boxes were all opened, the heaps of grain in the granary were raked with an iron rod, cooking pots were in-spected, a few spots were dug up, and in a few places the thatch was pulled out. But nothing suspicious was found; only a long thick lathi was seized. The body of a woman covered in an old straw mat was found under the eaves at the rear of the house, and it was produced before the daroga. Gobara Jena identified the body as that of the weaver woman, Saria. The daroga stroked his beard and said, "Well, Ramachandra Mangaraj, what do you have to say now? Do you remember the Doms of Ratanpur?"

The munshi added, "You thought all your problems had ended once that case had been heard."

Our own investigation has revealed that Mangaraj had prom-ised the daroga a bribe of one thousand rupees to send the Doms of Ratanpur to prison. But Mangaraj had not kept his promise. The daroga was now reminding him of this.

The inquiry began. The munshi untied his huge cloth bag and spread out the government papers. A china inkpot, stopped with a piece of cork tied to its neck, stood before him. With a rosewood-handle knife, the munshi sharpened a reed pen, testing it by scrib-bling on a small piece of paper. Then he wrote, "Help me, oh my guru! I surrender myself at the feet of Lord Jagannath, at the feet of Lord Baladev, Sri Rangaraj Mahaprabhu, Sri Gama Devati, and so on." Having written down the names of several gods and goddesses, he got down to the official business at hand. He wrote:

Plaintiff: The Mighty Government of the Company
Defendant: Ramachandra Mangaraj
Village: Gobindapur
District: Cuttack
Case: The murder of Saria, the weaver woman; the unlawful possession of her cow, Neta, and other valuables from her house.

In the meantime, the houses in the village were searched by the constables and the chowkidars. They came back, reporting that no male inhabitants had been found in the village. From what the women said, as they peeped through doors open only a crack, it was gathered that half the men in the village had left to visit relatives, half of the remainder were busy looking for cows that had wandered off, half of those left had gone to Puri for darshan of Lord Jagannath, and an equivalent number of people were responsible persons, appearing before the daroga and giving testimony. Since the villagers did not come out in droves, the daroga lost his temper and called them idiots, donkeys, fools, worthless fellows, and so on. This stream of invective sent shock waves through the village. The chowkidars swung into action, broke open doors, and beat people up. A man close to death's door might manage to save himself from the hands of Yama, the god of death, for a day or two, by lying swaddled in blankets, but no one can escape a policeman. One after another, all the men filed out of their houses. The testimony of thirty-two witnesses was recorded over two days. On the first day, two chowkidars took the body to Cuttack for the postmortem. The munshi Sahib wrote down the testimony of the witnesses, filling two and a half quires of handmade paper produced by jail inmates. Below are the statements of some of the witnesses, for your information.

Witness no. 1 for the Mighty Government of the Company:
Name: Gobara Jena
Father's name: Guhira Jena (deceased)
Caste: Pana
Age: Forty-five
Profession: Chowkidar
Village: Gobindapur
Subdivision: Balubisa
District: Cuttack.

Statement: "I keep watch over the village at night. Last night, while on duty, I heard Saria shouting from Mangaraj's backyard, 'Help me, he is killing me, help me.' It seemed to me that someone was beating her with a bamboo lathi."

When questioned, he replied, "No I did not see Mangaraj at the time." "But," he added, "I did hear his voice." As regards the cow, he stated, "This cow belongs to Saria, it is called Neta. I have seen it tethered in Mangaraj's courtyard for about a month now. I do not know how it got there." And he went on, "Mangaraj himself had it carried off."

Witness no. 2: Sana Rana.

When he appeared, he said he did not know anything about the case. The daroga became very angry and asked two of his constables to take him away. Half an hour later he was brought back, his hair disheveled, his body covered with dust, and his back and face marked by beatings. He said, "Huzoor, I will now tell you nothing but the truth."

Name: Sana Rana
Father's name: Bana Rana
Caste: Mali
Age: Thirty
Profession: Worshipper of the village goddess, and farmer
Village: Gobindapur
Subdivision: Balubisa
District: Cuttack.

Statement: "I know Saria. I do not know how she died. About a year ago, Mangaraj called me over one morning, through a farmhand, and took me into his grove. There, when we were all alone, he said, 'Look Sana, I am giving you a task and you must do it. If you do as I say, I will give you two acres of very good land for sharecropping. You will get two rupees extra to buy sweets.' I asked him what the task was. Saant said, 'You know Bhagia, the weaver. His wife Saria is barren. Everyday she prays at the feet of Goddess Budhi Mangala for a child. Go and tell her that the goddess has appeared to you in a dream and has told you that she, Saria, should offer puja at her abode, and that the goddess herself will then talk to her and bless her with a child.' After that, I met Bhagia and Saria on two or three occasions, and told them exactly what master wanted me to say. They listened attentively, but did not say anything. One afternoon, Bhagia took me to his house and asked me to tell him how the puja should be performed, what items would be required, how much the total cost would be and many other such things. I explained everything. I took ten annas and two paise from Bhagia to purchase items for the puja. One Saturday, after dark, Mangaraj, the barber Jaga, four farmhands carrying spades, and I, myself, arrived at the seat of Goddess Budhi Mangala. A big hole was dug behind the seat of the goddess, according to Mangaraj's instructions. Jaga hid in the hole, which was then covered over with leaves and twigs. Earlier in the morning, I had sent word to Saria and Bhagia to observe a fast. At midnight, when the village was quiet, I called them over and performed the puja. After placing the offerings before the goddess, I prayed to her. Bhagia and Saria, obeying my instructions, lay prostrate at the her feet. I prayed, 'Oh, mother Mangala! Grant Saria a favor. She has been worshipping you for such a long time. You have already blessed so many. Grant Saria a favor.' Jaga answered from inside the hole, 'Oh, my daughter Saria, you have been offering me puja for a long time. Every day you bow down to me on your way to the pond for a bath, and when you return, you offer me water and I receive it. I am pleased and I will grant you a favor: You will obtain a lot of money. Build me a temple. Come tomorrow morning to the weavers' ghat before washing your face. Dig at the spot where there are hibiscus flowers used in my puja. Take home whatever you find and offer me worship daily. I will give you bags full of such things from time to time. If you disobey me, I will wring Bhagia's neck and kill him.' Saria and Bhagia were trembling all the while in fear; they were unable to utter a word. I finished the puja, gave them some offerings, keeping the rest for myself, and took the two of them home. I saw Jaga come out of the hole, laughing. Then he and I buried a gold coin given us earlier by master at the weavers' ghat, threw some hibiscus flowers on the spot, and left for our homes. The next day I called on Bhagia and

Saria. When they saw me the couple broke into tears and asked, 'Tell us, where can we find money to build the temple?' On my advice they mortgaged their six and a third acres to Mangaraj and obtained the money. Later, the government jamadar came and pulled down Bhagia's house. Mangaraj's farmhands helped him. The jamadar stood watching as Mangaraj's farmhands carried off all of Bhagia's belongings. Since that day, Bhagia has gone mad and wanders the village. I heard Saria crying in Mangaraj's backyard for seven or eight days."

On being questioned he said, "I do not know how much money Mangaraj gave to Bhagia. I only know that when he took Bhagia to Cuttack to register the mortgage, he bought a sari for Saria. Mangaraj also unloaded twenty cartloads of stones near the seat of goddess Budhi Mangala for the construction of the temple. He gave me only four annas for the work I did for him, and no more. And I did not ask for any money, out of fear. That is all I know."

Signed Sana Rana.

Witness no. 3:
Name: Marua
Father's name: Lakshman Tihadi
Caste: Brahmin
Age: Unknown
Village: Gobindapur
District: Cuttack.

Upon cross-examination, the witness said, "I do not know what killed Saria. She had sat in our backyard for the last eight days. Day and night she sat in the same spot. Whenever she saw someone she would cry out, 'My six acres and a third, my six acres and a third, my Neta, my Neta,' and keep wailing. Whenever she saw

Saantani, she would cling to her feet. She would weep bitterly, and Saantani too would shed tears. On two or three occasions, Champa beat Saria with a broomstick and tried to chase her away. But Saria would not move. She did not take any food for eight days. Even when Saantani placed a portion of her own meal in front of her on a banana leaf she did not touch it; the food would be eaten by a dog or a cow. Sometimes she would eat a little bit, when Saantani sat beside her and pressed her to take some food. Saantani herself, too, had not taken any food for the last seven days. She wept every time she was asked to eat. So I did not press her to eat. On the seventh day of the fortnight, Saantani was taking an offering of rice to Goddess Budhi Mangala. When she heard Saria crying out, she placed the rice before her. Saantani came back home after this, and took to her bed. On the eighth day of the fortnight she passed away."

On being questioned further, Marua said, "I cannot say what killed Saantani. She had not been well since the eighth or tenth day after Snana Purnima. On Snana Purnima, Champa went somewhere riding in a palanquin. She was all smiles when she came back and said something to Saantani. Since that time, Saantani's condition worsened. She ate nothing at night; she took nothing during the day, either. She wept all the time. She flung herself at Saant's feet, entreating him to give Saria back her land. Saant took no notice of her appeal. Saantani did not utter a word after Champa abused her; she did not touch any food. Mukunda brought some medicine for her from the village doctor, but she would not take the medicine; she only touched it with her forehead and put it away."

Marua continued, "I have served in this house for the last ten years. My father's house is in a Brahmin quarter in Puri. My husband's name is Naganath Tiadi. I am told I was seven when I was married to a man who, at the time, was sixty-four. My husband sold his land and gave one hundred and sixty rupees to my father for the bride-price. At the time of the wedding, my husband suffered from asthma. This disease killed him. There was no one else in my husband's family. My father came, sold off all my husband's property, and brought me home. There I stayed for five to seven years. At that time, a holy man called Lalita Das lived in our village. I visited this holy man to listen to him narrating enchanting tales about Sri Chaitanya. My brothers became furious when they found out about these visits. I wanted to go away to Brindaban, so one night I escaped with the holy man; on the way, I stayed with him in Telenga Bazaar in Cuttack. Around that time, Saant was in Cuttack in connection with a court case. He brought me here."*

This O, Marua's signature, is the impression of her ring.

Witness no. 4:
Name: Baidhar Mohanty
Father's name: Dambaru Mohanty
Caste: Karana
Age: Fifty-six
Village: Kanakpur
Subdivision: Jankad
District: Cuttack.

---

*Certain parts of Cuttack's Telenga Bazaar neighborhood were known for prostitution in Senapati's time; cf. the reference to "the whores of Telenga Bazaar" in Senapati's story "Patent Medicine" (for a recent translation, see Fakir Mohan Senapati, *The Brideprice and Other Stories,* trans. K. K. Mohapatra, Leelawati Mohapatra, and Paul St-Pierre [New Delhi: Rupa, 2005]).

Statement: "I have been serving as the record keeper in the zamindari of Fatepur Sarasandha for the last twenty years. Previously, Keramat Ali of Midnapore was the zamindar. Now, the zamindar is Ramachandra Mangaraj of Cuttack; he acquired the zamindari on a mortgage basis."

The daroga put a number of questions to the witness, who for his part, gave several answers. We have, unfortunately, had to leave out many things, and are only able to provide a summary of his deposition.

Deposition of witness no. 4: "Mangaraj did not buy the zamindari with his own money; he paid for it with the rent money that he had collected. In the first year, Mangaraj collected the rent and gave it to Zamindar Dildar Mian. He collected the second installment of the rent and went to Midnapore. I accompanied him there. He told the zamindar, 'No rent could be collected because the former zamindar's family, the Bagha Singhs, told the tenants not to pay. What can be done? Tomorrow is the deadline for paying the revenue due the government.' Mangaraj then got the zamindar to sign a debt-deed and loaned him the money he had already collected from the zamindar's tenants. Now, because Sheikh Dildar Mian had borrowed money from him, Mangaraj collected interest on the loan from the tenants. This is what he did every time rent was paid to the government. In the end, Mangaraj bribed the officials working for the zamindar and got a debt-deed for thirty thousand rupees. Dildar Mian signed the deed in a drunken state. To take possession of the zamindari, Mangaraj did not have to travel all the way to Midnapore; he acquired the zamindari simply by filing a case in Cuttack.

Upon cross-examination, witness no. 4 said, "Yes, Mangaraj got Bhagia to mortgage six and a third acres of land to him. On the deed, it was mentioned that Bhagia had borrowed one hundred and fifty rupees. Until I consult the records, I am unable to tell you how much money was spent to write the deed, to get it registered, and so on." Then, he consulted the records and said, "Thirty-four rupees and ten annas."

The witness went on, "Yes, master filed a case against Bhagia in the law court in Cuttack. The notification, the decree, the warrant, and the proclamation of sale are all with me. None of these was given to Bhagia. The court messenger would come to Saant, take baksheesh from him, and take receipts for all the above-mentioned documents from me. I do not know how Saria died. This cow belongs to Bhagia."

Signed Baidhar Mohanty.

Witness no. 5:
Name: Champa
Father's name: I do not know
Caste: I belong to this house
Village: Gobindapur
District: Cuttack.

Statement: "I do not know Saria, she is not from this village. She did not die in our backyard; she died somewhere else, but her body lies here. She was ill with fever, and she died. Saant did not say anything to her. Our master is a very good man; he stays away from any kind of trouble. Saantani was ill with fever, and died. Heartbroken, I am unable to take food, I cry all the time. (The witness began to weep and then stopped abruptly, when the daroga threatened her.) The cow belongs to our house." (She added that it had been bought from Saria.)

O—*This impression of a ring is Champa's signature.*

The inquiry was adjourned, as it was already late in the night. The daroga, the munshi, and Gobara Jena, the chowkidar, consulted among each other far into the night. Suitable witnesses were collected, and in the morning the inquiry reconvened.

Witness no. 6:
Name: Bana Jena
Father's name: Dana Jena
Caste: Pana
Age: Eighteen
Occupation: Farmhand
Village: Makrampur
Subdivision: Balubisa
District: Cuttack.

Statement: "I know Saria well. I visited her house on several occasions. Her house is in Satutunia, in the Brahmin quarter. No, no, in the Pana quarter; no, no, in this village. Eight days ago, Ramachandra Mangaraj brought her here and hit her. He used this bamboo lathi (the witness held up a lathi). I saw Mangaraj hitting her at midnight on the twelfth day of this fortnight. He gave her twenty blows on her back. I had come out to look for cows belonging to the Sau family. My house is four miles away from here. I have never had any trouble with Saant. The chowkidar, Gobara Jena, is not my sister's husband."

I—*This sign of a stick is the signature of Bana Jena.*

Witness No. 7:
Name: Dhakei Jena
Father's name: Laguda Jena
Caste: Pana

Age: Unknown
Occupation: Farmhand
Village: Raitui
Subdivision: Balubisa
District: Cuttack.

Statement: "I saw the defendant, Ramachandra Mangaraj, hitting Saria with this bamboo lathi at midnight, on the ninth day of this fortnight. I had gone to buy some salt; then, I lay down on the verandah of the shop to sleep, as it was too late to go back home. When I heard the sound of blows, I climbed onto the thatched roof of the shop and looked out." (Correcting himself, "No, no, I climbed onto the roof of Mangaraj's house and looked out, and then I could see.") When asked about the cow, he said, "I recognize this cow. I have milked it many times. It is called Baula. This cow belongs to the weaver, Bhagia. Ramachandra Mangaraj stole it. He did so by digging a tunnel into Bhagia's house."

Upon cross-examination, he said, "Gobara Jena is not my mother's sister's son. He did not bring me here. I came on my own, to give evidence. He has not given me any food. I brought some rice flakes from home. The ninth day of this fortnight fell some twenty or twenty-two days ago. I cannot tell what day it is today according to the holy calendar."

I—*This sign of a stick is the signature of Dhakei Jena.*

Witness no. 8:
Name: Khatu Chand
Father's name: Nita Chand
Caste: Weaver
Age: Twenty-eight
Occupation: Weaving clothes

Village: Gobindapur
District: Cuttack.

Statement: "This is Bhagia's cow; Bhagia is my neighbor. The very day the government jamadar came and pulled down Bhagia's house, Mangaraj took this cow to his house. I do not know why he took the cow away. Mangaraj's farmhands helped demolish Bhagia's house and carried off all his household articles. Outside, Bhagia and Saria rolled in the dust, and howled. Because the government jamadar had come, we bolted our doors and remained inside. I looked out through a hole in my door and saw Gobara Jena calling me. I kept quiet. My wife told him I was not at home."

U—*This sign of a boat is the signature of Khatu Chand.*

Deposition of the accused.
Name: Ramachandra Mangaraj
Father's name: Dhani Nayak
Caste: Khandayat
Age: Fifty-two
Occupation: Zamindar
Village: Gobindapur
District: Cuttack.

Statement: "I did not kill Saria. Bhagia took money on loan from me. I took him to the law court and came into possession of his six acres and a third of land after winning the case. I took his cow to recover the costs of the case."

Signed Ramachandra Mangaraj.

Suddenly a madman appeared, a rag tied round his waist, his hair disheveled, and dust covering his body. In his hands, he held a drum. He broke into a wild sort of dance, shouting, "Saria, Saria!" The villagers were moved to pity, and lamented, "Oh, Bhagia! Was this fate written on your forehead?" When the madman caught sight of Mangaraj, he lunged at him to bite him. The chowkidars tried to stop him. When he struggled to break free, they tied him up on the daroga's orders.

The daroga finished his inquiry. In all, thirty-two witnesses were examined. All, except four, were allowed to return home.

Mangaraj was arrested and sent to the court in the early part of the morning. In handcuffs, surrounded on all sides by police constables, Mangaraj walked down the village path, a towel covering his lowered head. Villagers stood watching, as if they had assembled for a festival. The daroga led the party, and the munshi followed him. We cannot say if anyone in the village felt sorry for Mangaraj in his distress. Only Champa's pitiful wailing, "Oh, Saant, oh, Saant, where are you taking my Saant?" resounded down the village path. Saant looked back and asked her two or three times to go back home. The daroga and the munshi were soon fed up, but she would not listen to anyone. Her head was now uncovered, and she was out of breath from all her wailing. For about four miles, she followed Mangaraj like this, and at last said to him, "The white ants will eat the things in the store, the rats will destroy everything. What will happen now?"

This made Mangaraj stop. He took out two long tube-shaped keys. Putting these into her hands, he said, "Take good care of things, and do not worry." Champa tucked the two keys carefully away in the fold of her sari around her waist. "You must eat well," she said. "You must not neglect to take your meals." All along, Gobinda, the barber, had been beside her. Nobody heard Champa wail on her way back to the village.

Back at the police station the daroga, in consultation with the munshi, tailored the evidence of the witnesses. The four witnesses who had been brought along were given thorough instructions. After all this, the daroga sent the accused to the magistrate's court in Cuttack, accompanied by the report he had drawn up. We have managed to get a duly attested copy of it; if you like, you may read what it says:

Report of Daroga Inayat Husain

Your Lordship,

On the third day of this October, at eight o'clock in the morning, while this your humble servant was sitting in his office attending to government business, and while your obedient servant, Munshi Chakradhar Das, was sitting on his right side writing out his daily dairy, and while Constables Golam Kadir and Hari Singh were making their rounds, Gobara Jena, the chowkidar of Fatepur Sarsandha, which is under the jurisdiction of this police station, arrived and informed us that the weaver woman Saria, belonging to the above-mentioned area, had been murdered. Upon receiving this report, your humble servant communicated it to your office. The accused is a zamindar, a notoriously bad character and tyrant. Without wasting a minute, your servant set off for the spot to carry out the inquiry. He made a thorough search of the house of the accused, and arrested him, exercising great tact. The body of the woman, Saria, her belongings, and a white cow named Neta were seized from the house of the accused. A lathi, with which the accused had murdered Saria, was also seized. From the depositions made by four witnesses, it has been proven beyond all doubt that Ramachandra Mangaraj himself murdered Saria with this lathi. It has been firmly established that these four men were eyewitnesses to this murder, that the accused was a tyrant who took away the zamindari of an honest Muslim through trickery and deceit. In view of the above, it is clear that nobody but the accused committed the murder. I am therefore sending him to Cuttack to be produced before your Lordship. Your Lordship, you are my father and my mother, you are the Lord of this domain; may the mistakes in this report be graciously forgiven. Your humble servant knows that you will dispense justice to the parties concerned.

10 October 1831
Daroga Inayat Husain
Police Station, Kendrapada

The stolen goods seized from the house of the accused are being sent separately, in the custody of Constable Hari Singh. Your humble servant also hereby informs you that after the murder of Saria, her husband, Bhagia Chand, went mad and is harassing people. There is no one in the village to look after him. Therefore, he is also being taken before your Lordship.

Your most obedient servant,

———————————

CHAPTER TWENTY

Ram Ram Lala, the Lawyer

In one corner of the lockup of the Nazarkhana, enclosed by wooden railings on all sides, the accused sat leaning against a wall, his eyes closed. Alas, there was no one there to say a word to him. When everything is going well, everyone is a friend. People proclaim their loyalty to you when you are rich, but desert you when things get rough. Have you noticed that some people's doorsteps are overgrown with grass, while others' are crowded with people? Circumstances determine everything. An English poet once said, "a life without friends is like a world without sun." Man cannot live without friends.

"Greetings, Mangaraj." The accused looked up with a start. Many times in the past he had been addressed as respectfully, but today it was as if it breathed new life into him. Unable to utter a word, the prisoner stared at the figure in front of him. The visitor was a large man, his long arms reaching down to his knees. He wore a long-sleeved loose shirt, a chapkan stained with ink, and on his head was a turban made out of twenty-four arm-

172 / *Fakir Mohan Senapati*

lengths of embroidered fabric. Over his shirt was a length of Maniabandhi cloth printed with flowers, and he had put on a pair of Marathi shoes. A quill was tucked behind one of his ears; a full moustache hung down on either side of his mouth. One of his cheeks stuck out, since his mouth was stuffed with betel leaves. On seeing this figure, feelings of hope, trust, surprise, and doubt went through the mind of the accused; he was unable to say anything. He wondered who this person, who greeted him with such esteem and affection, could be. We presume that he must have been an old and true friend. It is on the strength of our knowledge of Chanakya that we have been able to arrive at such a conclusion. Chanakya says that people who stand by you at a king's court, or in a law court, or at a cremation ground, are your true friends. In other words, your true friends are lawyers in law courts and jackals skulking around cremation grounds.*

The accused did not have to spend a long time wondering. The constable, Gopi Singh, introduced the visitor, "Look, here is Ram Ram Lala, a famous lawyer in this court. Take his help. The Sahib values his words highly." At this, the lawyer looked very pleased with himself; he cleared his throat twice and said sweetly, like an old friend, "Mangaraj, you should have sent me word before this matter became so serious. True, almost all the lawsuits in the world are in my hands; clients do not leave me time even to spit. But when I heard your name mentioned, I came running." Mangaraj heaved a deep sigh and burst into tears, throwing himself at the feet of the visitor.

---

*The king's court in Chanakya's original Sanskrit treatise is equated here with a law court, and the narrator's translation also introduces the comparison of lawyers with jackals.

"Please get up, please," said Ram Ram Lala. "Leave everything to me and stay calm. There is nothing for you to worry about. Last night, I called on the Sahib at his residence. We talked about a number of cases. Had I known about yours, I could already have done wonders. I have found out everything about the case and have no doubt that all the accusations are absolutely false. These are all that evil-faced daroga's tricks. Soon you will see what I am going to do to him. Just let me have a word with the Sahib."

Mangaraj, his hands joined, exclaimed, "Lawyer Sahib! Tell me what to do! Save me! Save my life! You are my godfather! I am a child, I am helpless. I leave everything in your hands."

"You do not need to explain," said the lawyer. "I know everything, and I will do everything. But there is just one thing. This case is really serious, very serious. After all, it is a murder case. If you are not careful from the very beginning, you could go to the gallows. That evil-faced daroga is after your blood. You are a man of the world. Need I say more? You know everything about the ways of the law courts. There will obviously be expenses. You must not be afraid to spend money; you must not be close-fisted in this matter. Have you heard what the daroga is telling everyone? He says you are most surely going to hang. I am certain you agree that staying alive is what matters most. Tell me whether you have earned money, or whether money has earned you. Make your choice."

Mangaraj, who by now was weeping, answered, "Sir, how much money will you need? I do not have a single paisa with me now. And there is no one by my side at the moment. The daroga will not permit my record keeper and servants to come to see me, and talk to me. Please get me out of here, I will give you a thousand rupees when I get home."

At this point Constable Gopi Singh cut in, "Hey Mangaraj, your words make me wonder how you managed your zamindari. You think this a simple case of buying or selling, that you can postpone payment? The client says 'wait'; the lawyer says 'pay': 'First pay the money, then tell your story,' they say. Get the money if you want to win the case. Get the money. Lawyer Sahib, I cannot allow you to talk to the accused any longer. The Nazar ordered me to give you just enough time to exchange a few words with the accused. I am not alone here; there are four of us."

"Did you hear that, Mangaraj?" asked Ram Ram Lala. "It is not an easy job. You have to have everyone, from the constable to the judge, on your side. The case is so difficult that no other lawyer would dare take it, even if you offered ten thousand rupees. But, being the person I am, I have come forward. How can I abandon you now, when you have called me your godfather? All right, I myself will pay whatever is needed for your case. Not a paisa less than ten thousand rupees will be required. Mortgage your zamindari to me. It is not as if all these rupees will be needed at one time. As soon as you are acquitted, I will give you a detailed accounting of expenditures."

Mangaraj sat brooding for a while, a hand on his cheek. One crook can always spot another. Mangaraj knew only too well what mortgaging a property meant. However, a drowning man will clutch even at the tail of a tiger.

Lawyer Ram Ram Lala was extremely prompt when he had work to do; it took him a mere two hours to purchase the stamps, write out the mortgage deed, and get it registered. In the end, the lawyer Sahib said, "Mangaraj, stay inside the lockup and do not worry about anything. Now that I am here, I will sort everything out."

CHAPTER TWENTY-ONE

Cuttack Sessions Court

The Sessions Court in Cuttack was very crowded. People from all over—government offices, the bazaar, the weekly market—had come to witness the trial. Just as an audience gathers for a badi pala hours before the singers are ready, a crowd filled up the courtroom long before the trial was to begin. It was a large crowd, and there was a lot of noise. Two chaprassis were shouting, "Quiet! Quiet!," adding to the confusion. A powerful rural zamindar was being tried for murder. The magistrate had referred the case to the Sessions Court. The hearing had been going on for five days now, and today was to be the last. It had not yet started. Tomorrow was Wednesday, the day on which mail for England was dispatched. The judge Sahib was hurriedly writing a letter, which began, "My dear Lady." Whenever a criminal case was scheduled to be heard, the Sahib would open an English newspaper and read it, or leisurely write a letter, leaving everything else to the peshkar. All he did was sign the documents recording the depositions of the witnesses and pronounce the judgment. But today the Sahib was doing everything himself, because today's main witness was an Englishman; he would also have to write out the judgment in English. It was as if everything in the court today was Englished. But we are Oriyas, and so are our readers, and the printing presses here have only Oriya type. Thus, we have translated everything into Oriya.

The Sahib wet the envelope with a blob of spit and sent a peon off with it to the post office. Then he said, "Well, peshkar babu! Present the case." The government pleader, Isan Chandra Sarkar, Daroga Inayat Husain, and the lawyer for the defense, Ram Ram Lala, were present in the court.

The accused, Ramachandra Mangaraj, stood with joined hands in the dock behind wooden railings. On a chair to the right of the judge Sahib sat the doctor Sahib; he laid his hand on the Holy Bible and gave his evidence.

"My name is A. B. C. D. Douglas; Father's name: E. F. G. H. Douglas; Nationality: English; Age: Forty; Present residence: Cuttack. We are the civil surgeon for Cuttack district. On the eighth of this month, at 7:30 A.M., the postmortem of Saria's body was carried out in our presence at the government mortuary. Chowkidar Gobara Jena identified the body as that of Saria, and on the basis of that, we can state that it was Saria's body. What we found through our examination leads us to state with confidence that the death of Saria was not caused by any lethal weapon or similar object. We have enough evidence to conclude that she died after a long period of starvation and mental agony."

On being questioned by the judge Sahib, the witness stated, "There were no marks or wounds on the body; her blood seemed to have dried up. There was no blood in her heart. Her stomach was empty; there was no trace of anything in her bladder or intestines. All this tends to show that she died of starvation."

On being questioned by the government pleader, the civil surgeon further observed, "Yes, Gobara Jena did point out three marks on the back of the body. But after examining them thoroughly, we concluded that they were not caused by a beating; they looked like faint burn marks and could have been caused by a hot iron rod or similar object being applied to the back, after the death of the victim."

On further questioning by the government pleader, he acknowledged, "No, we did not ourself dissect the body. The native doctor, Gauranga Kar, and the compounder, Basudev Pattanayak, conducted the postmortem in our presence."

Further cross-examination vexed the witness, leading him to exclaim, "We have been a civil surgeon for over ten years now. Before this, we were in the military department. We studied medicine in London." And, he added, "We began as a hospital assistant and later were promoted during the Burmese war."

The judge Sahib now looked at the lawyer for the defense, and asked, "Do you have any questions?"

Ram Ram Lala, the lawyer for the defense, looked at the doctor, and asked, "Did you find any marks on the victim's back from the lathi now presented as evidence in this court?"

The judge Sahib interrupted, "This is nonsense. Do you have any other questions?"

The lawyer for the defense changed his question: "You say that Saria died of starvation. Did she starve herself, or did the accused force her to starve?"

The judge Sahib cut in, "All right, continue, you may continue." The cross-examination proceeded.

"Is there any evidence that Saria died in front of the house of the accused?"

The judge Sahib lost his temper, "If you ask more such irrelevant questions, I will cancel your lawyer's license!"

"Oh, my Lordship," replied the lawyer for the defense, "you are my father and my mother, you are the Badshah of this world."

After the accused had been cross-examined, a heated debate ensued between the lawyers representing the two sides, lasting two and a half hours. While this was going on, the judge Sahib managed to finish a four-foot long newspaper and his midday meal. Had he not ordered them to stop, the lawyers would have talked on and on.

As per the orders of the judge, the head clerk prepared the summary of the proceedings, filling over twelve pages. It took three days for the summary to be written out and filed. We have been able to procure an attested copy of the document; however, since we have been giving brief summaries of everything we reproduce here only a synopsis, which will inform the reader about the case.

At the Sessions Court of Cuttack District,
H. R. Jackson Esq.,
Sessions Judge, presiding.
Under the authority of the East India Company,
Orissa Division, Cuttack.

The Government versus Ramachandra Mangaraj
Village: Gobindapur
Subdivision: Asureswar
District: Cuttack.

Case: The murder of Saria, the wife of a weaver, and the looting of her household articles.

From the papers relating to this case and the arguments made by the lawyers, it is clear that this is a criminal matter. The district magistrate sent the accused, charged with murder, to the Sessions Court. The police produced eight witnesses in support of their case. Having very carefully and attentively examined the depositions of the witnesses, and also, having heard the arguments of the lawyers, we have concluded that the accused did not murder Saria by hitting her with a lathi, as the police have submitted. Her death was due to starvation over a long period, and mental agony. The main evidence enabling us to arrive at such a conclusion is the testimony of the civil surgeon, the principal witness in this case. He emphatically observed that there were no marks of beating on the body.

The evidence put forward by the witnesses has convinced us that the police case was, in fact, a frame-up. We have reason to believe that Gobara Jena, who filed the First Information Report, is at the root of it all. If we compare his F.I.R. with his deposition in the witness box, it is clear that he made a great effort to pass falsehood off as truth, but that he has not been able to defend his case under hard questioning. The so-called eyewitnesses Bana Jena and Dhakei Jena, who claimed to have seen the accused murder Saria with a lathi, are relatives of the chowkidar, Gobara Jena. Besides, they live four miles away from the house of the accused. Therefore, it would not have been possible for them to be awake at midnight and to see what the accused was doing at that hour. Again, the map provided by the police makes it clear that there were three row of houses between the spot where the accused is said to have killed Saria and the point from where the witnesses say they saw him do it. It would manifestly have been impossible for the witnesses to see through the houses. Other circumstantial evidence and the confused replies given by the witnesses during cross-examination give us enough reason not to believe them. These wretched creatures do not realize the consequences of what they have been induced to do. They have been duped on account of their simple rustic nature and by the counsel of evil men. On close scrutiny, we find that Gobara Jena has repeatedly told lies. We therefore order that criminal proceedings be instituted against him.

The police have produced witnesses to prove that the accused was a bad character. All we have been able to gather is that the accused took away other people's property by clever and devious means. But, there is no evidence that he used unlawful force against anyone. Therefore, it is impossible to believe that such a person could commit a murder. Besides, we have not found any motive for such an act.

The police have seized from the house of the accused, items belonging to Saria and Bhagia Chandra. These include a weaver's comb, a few spindles, other equipment for weaving, and a few pots and pans. However, from the list submitted by the accused in the Civil Court, it appears that Bhagia Chandra had mortgaged to him six and a third acres of land. It seems that, in order to recover the expenses incurred for the civil suit, the accused acquired the above-mentioned items at auction. Of course, it must be stated that mortgaging the land, winning the case, and auctioning the property were all accomplished through deceit. Nonetheless, all this is irrelevant in the present case. We have reason to believe that because the accused took away Bhagia

Chandra's rent-free six and a third acres, and looted all his belongings, Bhagia went mad with grief and Saria died of starvation. But, all this is not enough to convict the accused of murder.

The police have also seized from the house of the accused, a white cow named Neta. The parties in the case agree that the cow belongs to Bhagia Chandra. The accused claims that he bought it at the public auction of Bhagia Chandra's property that was ordered by the court to recover expenses incurred for his civil suit. But this is definitely a lie, since there is no mention of the cow Neta in the papers placed before me carrying the seal of the Civil Court and relating to the auction. We now have enough evidence to believe that the accused acquired other people's property through deceit. He began life as a man of little consequence, but he has amassed great wealth through dishonest means. And he took the said cow, on the presumption that Bhagia was weak and defenseless. In view of all these facts, we hereby pronounce the following verdict:

> The accused, Ramachandra Mangaraj, is absolved of the murder charge, but he is hereby sentenced to six months of rigorous imprisonment, and ordered to pay a fine of five hundred rupees for unlawfully taking away the cow. Nonpayment of the fine will result in an extra three months of rigorous confinement.
>
> *17 May 1832*
> *H. R. Jackson*
> *Sessions Judge*

The court concluded its business for the day. The judge Sahib's buggy left; four constables handcuffed the accused and led him out of the Nazarkhana with the jail warrant. Lawyer Ram Ram Lala was sitting under the banyan tree in front of the court.

Upon seeing the accused, he called out, "Mangaraj, did you see how hard I fought for you before the judge Sahib? I saved you from the gallows. Do not worry. Go merrily into prison. Before you have pressed even one pot of oil, I will get you out through an appeal to the Supreme Court."

We have definite information, however, that no effort was made to file such an appeal.

CHAPTER TWENTY-TWO

Gopi Sahu's Shop

Gopalpur ghat, on the bank of the Birupa, was where people took the ferry on their way to Cuttack. Previously, the village of Gopalpur had stood on this spot, but it washed away in a flood on the eighth day of Bhodua in the eighth year of the reign of the kings of Puri. Although the village as such no longer existed, its name still survived.

A huge banyan tree grew on the river bank. Gopi Sahu's shop, seven arm-lengths by five, stood under it. The shop had one room, enclosed by three walls, and a verandah, two arm-lengths long. If by chance a wayfarer stayed the night, he would cook his meal on the verandah.

Gopi had grown old and was no longer able to work in the fields; he had grown weaker after his wife died. His sons did not ask him to do any work, but Gopi was not a man to sit idle. Doing something was better than doing nothing. Last year, he had found a way to keep himself busy. Every morning after eating a handful of rice, he would come to his shop, stay there until evening, then lock the doors with a pipelock and return to his house, one mile away.

In his shop, he stocked rice, dal, salt, rice flakes, tobacco, and so on. Every evening he would put them in a basket and carry them home. Gopi told people that lately he had become extravagant. Unless he took a pinch of opium he could not sleep, and after the opium he would take a handful of flaked or puffed rice. He had also started smoking tobacco. Of course, he paid for all this from his own earnings. He had started his shop with a capital of eight annas that his sons had given him. He met his expenses from the few paise profit he made in the shop, and his capital remained untouched.

It was the month of Aswina. The sky remained overcast all day; there had already been two or three rain showers. The rain kept falling, the road was muddy; there was no sign of any wayfarers. It was still some time before evening, but because the sky was cloudy it had already become dark. Gopi looked at his shop, and remarked, "I have not been able to sell even a paisa's worth of tobacco today." Then he put all the articles from the shop in a basket, tied a towel around his head, sat down on the verandah, and thought to himself, looking up at the sky, "Evening has not yet arrived." He looked toward the river ghat, perhaps in hope that a traveler might yet appear. With his gaze fixed on the ghat, he started singing a bhajan:

The day is done
And I have spent it without
A song for the Lord,
Like a river
Years of life flow into the ocean

Never to return.
Drunk with worldly desires
Man forgets his real home in heaven.
O Lord, be kind to this wretched being
Day and night your name shall I sing.

"Hey, shopkeeper, can we spend the night here?" Startled, Gopi looked up and saw two travelers, a man and a woman, standing in front of him. The man had wound a length of silk cloth around his head; he carried a small bundle on his back and held a palm-leaf umbrella over his head. The woman had draped herself in an expensive silk sari, with an elaborate border. Only her nose jewel, in the shape of a dancing peacock, was visible. People say you are judged by how you dress. So, seeing these travelers, Gopi was convinced that they were very rich. He hurriedly stepped down, and saluted them, saying, "Please come in. Come into my shop. You can cook your meals here. I will get you everything you need." Seeing their soiled feet, he gave them water in two tumblers to wash. Then he spread out a tattered leaf mat in the tiny room. The woman washed her feet, changed her wet clothes, and sat cross-legged on the mat. Impressed by her ornaments, Gopi kept calling them "Master" and "Mistress." The humility and deference shown her pleased the woman very much. From the end of her sari she took out a four-anna coin and threw it toward Gopi, saying, "Here, dear man, bring us some food to cook for our evening meal." Gopi picked up the coin, looked it over two or three times, and then tucked it into a fold in the cloth wrapped around his waist, near his navel. If you had seen Gopi, you would have guessed he was telling himself, "I wonder whose face I saw first thing this morning? I have already got four annas before even selling anything; that has never happened to me before." He brought out everything for the meal: rice, unhusked black gram, and salt. He put them in front of the travelers and started making a fire in the firehole. The woman began to cook the rice, and the man picked up a pitcher in his left hand and went out to fetch water. The woman asked Gopi, "Can I get some milk and ghee? I do not enjoy my food without them."

"You are right, Mistress, absolutely right," said Gopi, "I know the awful things I have given you are not fit for your palate. A breakfast for your ladyship would have fine clean flaked rice, fresh milk, clean molasses, and fresh jaggery from the south; and for your midday meal, two seula or balia fish, green bananas, green gram, and, of course, milk and ghee. But what can I find in this part of the country, where only beggars live? It is a stroke of luck that the dust from your lotus feet fell on my head today. Give me a few more paise, and I will go about the village to see if I can get anything."

The woman threw him another four-anna coin. Gopi tucked it in the fold of his cloth, as he had done earlier, and hurried toward the village. A few hours later, his youngest son, Brundaban, brought some ghee in a banana leaf cup, a half-seer of milk in a clay pot, and a couple of brinjals. Putting these on the shop verandah, he called out, "Sir, father has sent you this; he could not come himself, because he cannot see in the dark."

There was now no one else in the shop. The woman was busy cooking and the man was helping her. They started talking.

"Did you hear what people said, Gobinda?" said the woman. "Did you pay attention? Everyone called me 'Mistress.' Wherever I went, people addressed me as 'Mistress.' Has anyone ever called you 'Master' before? Come to Cuttack with me, come. I will show you what I can make of you. I am tired of having had to explain things to you for the past four days."

"No, Madam," replied Godinda. "Let us go back to our village and live there. We will buy land and farms, keep farmhands and grow crops."

"Oh, people are right when they say, 'The mind of a barber is as useless as a dark night.' Tell me, what is the point of owning land? What I have taken will last one hundred, no two hundred years."

"I do not agree," the man retorted. "I want to go back to my village. I have not had any news from there for a long time now; I am feeling anxious and worried. If you do not want to go with me, give me my share, then do whatever you like."

"Your share? What share? Whose share?" cried Champa, for that was who the woman was. "Now I know why people say, 'Some people eat cake, while others eat cow dung and think it is cake.' The money was mine before, and it is mine now. Was it not I who stole it? For seven days now, you have been dragging me from door to door, from village to village, in the rain, through the mud, and I am almost dead from fatigue. Now tell me, who buried gold coins, machine-minted coins, and gold ornaments in three different places in Saant's bedroom? In the dead of night, I dug a hole, and Saant and I buried them. Did you know anything about that? Now tell me, does all this belong to you or to me?"

"All right, that was your work. But what could you have done without the keys? Who told you to get hold of the keys?" asked Gobinda.

"Oh, you are so proud of such a silly suggestion," answered Champa. "What a great idea! As if I could not have hit upon that myself! You saw how I followed Saant for four miles, on hot sand,

and got blisters all over my feet! I cried myself hoarse that day, and yet you want to take credit for everything! You think you are so clever. Have you forgotten how I spent the night at the Brahmin widow's house, made friends with her, and took the title deed out of her alcove? Was it you who taught me how to do that? Hah!"

Gobinda did not say anything more. He went out and sat sulking on the verandah. Champa, too, did not utter a word. Both had learned the same tricks at the same school, both were crafty and cunning. Each was a match for the other, and neither would yield; they knew each other only too well. Champa was worried that once back in the village, the money and the gold would get into barber Gobinda's hands and be impossible to pry loose. Besides, there were his mother and wife to worry about. For his part, Gobinda was sure that once Champa reached Cuttack, she would definitely slip out of his clutches. A she-dog that lived by licking leftover food from leaf-plates would certainly discard the old one and run to lick the new one thrown to her. Two persons of equal strength pulling in opposite directions do not budge.

Night had fallen. The meal of rice and dal was ready. Champa stood quietly for some time. Then she went close to Gobinda, saying sweetly, "Listen, Gobinda. You say your home is eight miles on the other side of the river. All right, first come with me to Cuttack; there, I will give you some money, and you can visit your home. If you do not do as I say, I will not give you a single paisa, not even the water in which the coins and gold are washed. Come, come, we are starving. We should eat."

Gobinda was very hungry, perhaps that was why he was willing to accept her terms and why he was getting up. But it was dark, and Champa could not see anything. Getting no answer, she lost her temper. "Oh, go to hell! If a slave is called a Lord, he wants to dance on your head. Go, get lost, what do I care whether you eat or starve."

Gobinda sat back down angrily, and glared at Champa. He thought to himself, "All right, I am a slave and you are a queen!" But he kept his mouth shut. All his great dreams of large farms vanished in an instant. All day he had been walking through rain and mud, and he was very tired and hungry. Until now he had sat brooding, but when he heard Champa call him a slave, he felt as if a scorpion had stung him. He was inflamed with anger, but he did not say anything, for he knew even two of him would not be able to overpower her. Many a time, with his own eyes, he had seen Champa give a good beating to strong and hefty farmhands. His anger smoldered like an ember burning under a heap of dry grass.

Champa set out two leaf-plates piled with rice. In the middle of each she made a hollow and poured in some dal. Making sure Gobinda was not watching, she emptied into her own plate the pot of milk that Brundaban had brought. But, sitting in the dark, Gobinda saw her do this and felt as if his whole body were on fire. He wondered what this woman would do with money and gold, if this was what she did with a pot of milk!

Champa called out, "Hey, here is your rice. Eat it or not, do as you like. I cannot keep begging you to come and eat."

Champa wiped her face with her wet hand, sat on the floor, and began to swallow huge balls of rice making slurping noises. In a minute her plate was empty. She washed her mouth, looked out, and called Gobinda again, "Hey, come and have your food."

But there was no reply. She got annoyed and said, "I think this good food is not for beggars like you." Her words fell like straw into a raging fire.

Champa spread out half the cloth covering the bundle they had carried with them, and lay down on her back, taking care to keep the bundle close to her neck. Gobinda sat brooding on the verandah. He knew how difficult it is to snatch a gem away from a snake if it carries the gem on its hood. The people of the village of Gobindapur have told us that Gobinda had expected Champa to behave differently. A man expects respect, love, devotion, and loyalty from a woman; Champa's conduct made it clear that although she had taken a fancy to Gobinda, he would always remain nothing more than a barber to her. As he sat brooding over this, Gobinda lost all track of time.

The night was very dark, so dark you could not even see your own hand. A southerly wind whistled through the trees. Rain fell in squalls. A banyan tree formed a dark solid mass, producing fearful sounds as it swayed in the wind. A few black bats flitted about in the night, and then attached themselves to the dark mass of the tree. Others flew off into the sky. Some made screeching noises as they bit into the fruit of the banyan tree, dropping a few on the ground below. In the midst of all these eerie noises, Champa's snores sounded strangely terrifying. Two animals biting and snarling at each other near the banyan tree made Gobinda start, and he looked up. The lamp burning in the room was now growing feeble, its last light, like the last red rays of the setting sun, fell across the floor. Gobinda watched two jackals fight over a few pieces of fruit from the banyan tree, one driving the other off and grabbing everything for itself. He saw this, and it told him something. He thought for a while, then stood up and glanced around. Quietly entering the room, he looked Champa over from head to foot. He had put his barber's pouch in a recess in the wall. He reached for it, opened it, and took something out. Slowly, he approached Champa, staring intently at her, just as a leopard watches a sleeping sow. There was fire in his eyes, and in his right hand, he grasped the object firmly. He was so tense and careful, he did not even breathe. As he put his right foot forward a flash of light swept across Champa's body and the wall. Startled, he drew back and stepped off the verandah. He looked around anxiously, but could hear nothing except the same eerie sounds as before. A few black bats flapped their wings and flew off the lower branches of the tree. The jackal, which was feeding, skulked away. A ray of light caught the object in Gobinda's hand. Now he understood why there had been the flash of light. With more courage than he had mustered before, Gobinda stepped stealthily back into the room, and just as the leopard attacks the sow, he pounced on Champa. At this moment, the lamp went out, its wick flickering before sinking into the bottom of the lamp. Nothing more was visible. There was a piercing scream, and the sound of someone furiously beating against the earthen floor. After a time everything in the room became still. Outside, the bats flapped their wings noisily and flew about the tree. A gust of wind shook the trees and swept their branches toward the shop. For a while, in that blind darkness, it seemed that the world was coming to an end.

CHAPTER TWENTY-THREE

The Law of Karma

Near Gopalpur the riverbed was very wide, at least a mile across. It was not full of water, however, and where the river was narrow, it was very deep. The water flowed near the southern bank, and at the ghat, on the northern bank, there was only sand. Only during flooding did water come up to the ghat. Since there had been very little rain over the previous ten to twelve days, the bed was mostly dry. But now, lumps of foam were floating toward the ghat, for it had been raining nonstop since the day before yesterday. Here and there, a lump, the size of a pumpkin, broke into pieces as it got sucked into a whirlpool. No one could keep count of the twigs, pieces of straw, and other things drifting by. The river was very deep here, and infested with crocodiles. People did not dare wade in above their knees, because the crocodiles became more dangerous when the river flooded. The villagers believed that the foam made the crocodiles angry, and so they feared the flood waters that brought it.

All during the day, a boat was moored at the ghat. The villagers and vendors used it to cross the river; the boatman lived in a shed nearby, and he ferried across the government mail. For this, he got two rupees a month. But, the villagers did not pay him cash: during harvest time, he collected a sheaf of corn from each household, and on market days, the vendors gave him a few dried fish, a couple of brinjals, a little salt, and a small amount of oil. On the days that he ferried an important merchant or an unknown traveler, he got a paisa or a half to "buy sweets." His earnings varied according to place, time, and person. When a government man such as the daroga, the munshi, or a kanugoi crossed the river in his boat, he would, without fail, receive a box on the ears, a slap on the face, and some choice abuse. The boatman, Chandia Behera, claimed that he had spent all his life ferrying people across the river and that no other boatman did this better than he.

It was very late. All through the night there had been storms and heavy rain. Now, the wind and rain had ceased, but the sky remained overcast. A few stars peeped through occasional cracks in the clouds. A traveler, carrying a small bundle on his back, wandered along the bank. He would walk a few hundred paces beyond the ghat and then return. Our guess is that he desperately wanted to cross to the other bank, even swimming if necessary, but that his courage kept failing him. He stood at the ghat and shouted, "Oh, brother boatman! Oh, brother boatman!" Chandia Behera was sleeping on the sand near the ghat. He had tied his boat to a pole that he had driven into the riverbed. The traveler anxiously repeated, "Oh, brother boatman! Oh, brother boatman!" and suddenly looked over his shoulder, as if he were frightened of something. Was the boatman fast asleep? Why was he ignoring the repeated calls? We, of course, know that the boatman always got up before dawn. The authors of the Shastras advise one to leave one's bed before sunrise; it was not out of obedience to the Shastras, however, that Chandia was awake at this hour. Since the government mail arrived in the small hours of the night on some days of the week, he had to be awake to ferry it across. The ghat became empty soon after sunset, so he would eat a little and go to sleep early. After all, how long can one lie asleep?

Chandia crouched in front of a fire with his head on his knees, warming his hands. Perhaps he was wondering who this traveler was, who had arrived at such an unusual hour. He was definitely not a government man, because he called him "brother." Whoever it was, let him go on calling; he would wait until it was light. Again the traveler shouted, "Oh, brother boatman, please come out. I will give you money to buy sweets."

Chandia could keep quiet no longer; the mention of money to buy sweets made him cough two or three times. No doubt, there is some magical power in the sound of the words "money to buy sweets," which never fails to bring a person under its spell. Bigger men, much bigger than a poor boatman, cough at the sound of these enchanting words. Chandia replied from within his shed, "Who is calling? Wait until light. I will not come out now even if you pay me a lakh of rupees."

The traveler shouted back, "Look, brother boatman, I have to go to Cuttack for a court case. I have to get there early. Take five rupees."

Five rupees! What was that? Five rupees for ferrying just one passenger? Never before in all of Chandia's life had something like this happened. We doubt very much if he had ever got all of five rupees at any one time. A moment ago, he vowed he would not come out of his shed even if paid one lakh of rupees, but now perhaps he did not consider it necessary to calculate the difference between five rupees and a lakh. He was worried that the traveler might go away or might give him only a paisa or two once day broke. With this in mind, Chandia called out from the shed, "All right, wait. I am coming."

He blew into the fire and lit a kahali; then he picked up an oar and went out. He pulled his clothes tightly around his waist, wound a towel around his head, and covered it with a palm-leaf toupee. He said to the traveler, "All right, give me what you want. I got up only because it was you; I would not have budged for someone else."

The traveler gave him five rupees. The boatman counted the money three times to himself, "One, two, three, four, five." It is said, "Count your money before you accept it, and strain the water before you drink it." The boatman sucked hard at his kahali, and when it was lit, he took a good look at the coins in its light. Then he carefully tucked the coins into a fold in the cloth around his waist. He looked up and saw the sky was getting light. Meanwhile, the traveler had already seated himself in the stern of the boat. The boatman warned the traveler, "Sit tight." With his right hand, he touched the boat and then his forehead three times prayerfully. He untied the boat and jumped into it, crying, "Victory to Mother Ganga!"

The currents were very strong, and they swept the boat downriver before the boatman could use his oar. Day had almost broken by the time they had, with much difficulty, crossed nearly one-third of the way, and at that moment someone on Gopalpur ghat started singing,

Ram and Lakhman went to hunt the deer;
At the hut a mendicant appeared
And said, "Sita give me alms
Or else a curse will fall on Ram."

Sitting tight in the boat, the traveler kept looking back nervously toward the ghat. When, through the darkness, the song reached his ears, he became restless and edgy, and stood up. The boat started to rock. The boatman, busy rowing, had not yet heard the song, and rudely told him to sit down. The traveler's anxious expression made the boatman look back toward the ghat, and he cried out, "Oh, God! It's the government mail carrier." Saying this, he set about turning the boat around.

The traveler became distraught, imploring the boatman, "Oh, brother, do not take the boat back. Please. First ferry me to the other bank."

The boatman answered him, "What a silly thing to say! Can I avoid government work? Do you want me to go jail?"

The night had come to an end, and it had become light. The boatman suddenly noticed the traveler was stained all over with blood: there was blood on his clothes, blood on his hands, and blood on his bundle. Shocked, he exclaimed, "Hey you, where did the blood come from? Have you murdered someone?"

The traveler grabbed his bundle and jumped into the river while the boatman cried, "Stop, stop!" Before he could swim fifteen to twenty feet, a Gomuhan crocodile swam up and caught him in its jaws. The bundle floated some distance and then sank. Chandia was left staring, "Who was this man? Where did he come from? Where did he want to go?"

You see, dear reader, we are the author, and therefore we are omniscient. We know why this crocodile snatched the man away, where it carried him, whether it treated him well or not; we have answers to all these questions. However, we are unwilling to talk about this openly since Chandia Behera himself kept the story a secret for reasons best known to him. When the man jumped off the boat into the river, a bunch of palm-leaf pages fell inside the boat. Chandia kept these in his shed. A few days later, he asked one of his passengers, a village teacher, to read them. They went as follows:

"In the seventh year of the reign of Sri Sri Mukunda Dev, on the afternoon of the second day in the dark fortnight of the month of Kumbha, this deed is written out in the presence of Ramachandra Mangaraj, the zamindar and moneylender of Gobindapur, by me, Sama Sahu, the oilman of the same village. I hereby declare that Mangaraj will be entitled to take from my barn, in the month of Dhanu, paddy at the rate current at that time."

For many days after the incident, Chandia, as he rowed his boat, would stop and look at the spot where the man had jumped into the river.

CHAPTER TWENTY-FOUR

Inquiry into a Death

It was early in the morning, and today, it was not raining. Gopi Sahu arrived at his shop, his head covered with a knotted and tattered towel. On his shoulder he carried the shop's wares in a basket. He had the key in his hand. He unlocked the shop and looked in. What he saw stunned him. He stood petrified. Something had happened, something he had neither heard nor seen: on the floor, a woman lay dead, her eyes staring at the ceiling. The whole room was spattered with blood: there was blood on the firehole, blood on the leaf-plate, blood on the rice pot. Blood had spurted and sprayed patterns on the wall. Gopi ran home to tell the other villagers. They rushed to the shop to see what had happened. The village chowkidar, Santia Jena, immediately ran to the Balabasti police station in Makrampur, three miles away, to file a report. The jamadar there, Sheikh Torab Ali, and Constable Pitu arrived at the scene of the crime in the afternoon. Sheikh Torab Ali had the reputation of being strict; the very mention of his name made people tremble in fear; even pregnant cows moved to one side to make way for him. The jamadar Sahib covered his nose and his beard with a piece of cloth and began to inspect the body. The corpse was that of a woman wearing a silk sari, with a few gold and silver ornaments on her hands and neck. A blood-stained razor lay near her throat, which had been slashed like a hen's ritually slit by a Muslim. The corpse had already begun to decay. Swarms of flies buzzed over it like bees in a hive. Its tongue stuck out, its teeth were bared, its eyes were wide open as if staring at the ceiling, its hair was disheveled and sticky with blood. On both sides of the corpse, there was blood, four fingers deep; it was turning black and gave off an offensive smell. The cheeks of the body were swollen like two ou fruit, and its bloated belly was round like a barrel. It seemed as if someone had cut her throat after pinning her face down under his foot and grabbing her by the hair. She had kicked desperately while being killed and left deep marks in the earthen floor. The jamadar Sahib could not stand the stench and sight of the corpse for long, and left the room. Outside, in his great wisdom, he came to the conclusion that this was most certainly a murder case, and not a case of dacoity, for otherwise no ornaments would have been left on the body. At the jamadar's orders, two scavengers tied a rope to the feet of the corpse and dragged it to the bank of the river. As it was being dragged out, the silk sari slipped off and the body looked even more gruesome. The jamadar had the ornaments removed and put them in a bag to be forwarded to the government. The anklets would not come off, so the scavengers hacked off the feet to remove them.

The inquiry began the morning of the next day. Chowkidars from five neighboring villages and constables went out and rounded up the suspects. The jamadar Sahib took his seat under the banyan tree and commenced the inquiry. Three or four hundred suspects had already been brought before him, and there were still a few more. Every suspect was made to sit beside the corpse. In the meantime it had swollen to four times its size, its tongue now as big as a banana flower. The stench was indescribable. This was the naked body of a woman, with no feet. How had she walked? Was she a demoness? The suspects could not bear to sit near the corpse for long. Driven by the stench, and fear, they hurried back to report before the jamadar.

The jamadar's kacheri was in session under the banyan tree. Ten or fifteen vultures sat on the sands of the riverbed, watching intently, and a few more flew in to join them. Ten or fifteen jackals and dogs gathered nearby. A fight broke out among some dogs over one of the hacked-off feet. A short distance away, the other foot was being picked at by vultures. A jackal broke into their midst, suddenly snatching it away. The vultures pulled back a little and sat with their wings outspread. Their nostrils covered with twists of cloth, four scavengers were kept busy driving off the dogs and vultures with lathis. The jamadar had already recorded the depositions of a large number of suspects.

Gopi Sahu, the old shopkeeper, said, "Your eminence! Three-quarters of my life is already over, there's only one quarter left. Am I going to tell a lie at my age? Today is ekadasi, and I have fasted since morning. I swear by the sacred basil plant that I know nothing about this incident. I have been ill for the last six months and have never come to my shop during this time."

Chandia, the boatman, said that due to the rain and the storm no one had crossed the river and that he had not gone to the river bank for the last four days. The depositions of many villagers were taken down by the jamadar.

It was getting dark. Everyone in the village had given testimony; everyone had been thoroughly interrogated. The jamadar Sahib and his two constables were debating whether they should continue the inquiry the next day, or end it here and now. While this was going on, the droppings from a kite on a branch above fell on the jamadar's beard, whitening half of it. Crying "Toba, Toba!" the jamadar jumped to his feet, looking up at the kite and angrily calling it an idiot, an ungrateful wretch, and so on. The chowkidars lent him their support and hurled abuse and stones at the kite. It took three buckets of water to wash the jamadar's long beard clean. He now set about closing the inquiry, saying to the people present, "Nobody knows this woman; perhaps she was a wayfarer. No one murdered her. This is a case of snake-bite."

Gopi Sahu, the shopkeeper, added by way of evidence, "Oh, justice incarnate! This place is infested with snakes. The flood has brought thousands of snakes here from somewhere. The fear of these snakes drove people away from the village, and the place became deserted. I came to my shop yesterday and saw a huge cobra, and I ran away in fear."

The chowkidar, Muturu Malik, submitted, "Oh, justice incarnate! There are many snakes here. When I went to pay my respect to your Lordship last time, I saw fifteen cobras sleeping under this tree, and I ran away in fear."

Budhei Dhapal Singh, the chowkidar of Mugupur, said that he had seen a tampa snake near the doorway of the shop while the woman was sleeping inside.

The jamadar recorded the evidence given by everyone present. He prepared a report saying that a beggar woman from the west country had been seen begging for alms; it was she who died of snake bite in the village of Gopalpur. The report mentioned that there were several snake-bite marks on her body. The report further stated that no suspicious circumstances surrounding the woman's death had been found. The jamadar sent this report on to the daroga of Kendrapada and thus disposed of the case. The usual gifts for the daroga and the munshi of the Kendrapada police station accompanied the large envelope containing the report. By order of the jamadar, four scavengers tied a rope around the neck of the corpse, dragged it to the bank, and flung it into the river. The boatman, Chandia, saw a crocodile come up and take the corpse, as it floated down the river to the same spot where a crocodile had carried off his passenger earlier.

While crossing the river the jamadar remarked to one of his constables, "See, such a serious case, but it did not bring us even two hundred rupees." The constable replied, "God is all powerful. He gives according to his mercy."

After that day, Gopi Sahu never went to his shop. In the month of Kartika, it rained for three days on end, and the shop collapsed. The path running past it was not used any more. Boatman Chandia shifted his shed from Gopalpur to a spot near Haripur, about a mile downstream. During the day, let alone at night, no one dared visit Gopalpur ghat. Many saw the huge ghost of a woman sitting on the banyan tree and shaking its branches; sometimes the ghost would go to the riverbed at midday and scatter sand to the winds. The ghat was no longer called Gopalpur ghat; it was known as the Abode of the Ghost.

CHAPTER TWENTY-FIVE

The Mangaraj Household

What do these six and a third acres represent? It is said that the Kohinoor, the world-famous diamond, destroyed every family that owned it. The fate of kings from Allauddin to Ranjit Singh is shining proof of this. And yet, ever since this jewel has adorned the crown of our highly revered, greatly honored empress of India, who dwells in the White Island and who is manifest like our goddess Kamala, the fame and power of England have spread all over the globe. The poison that kills everyone else glows around the throat of Lord Mahadeba, the God of gods, and expresses his supreme divinity. The point of this is that nothing in its rightful place is ever a source of trouble. Forget about big things, consider our small plot of land, measuring six acres and a third. People said that in all of Gobindapur, it would be hard to come by as fertile a plot. Yet this piece of land was a destroyer of families: it ruined the Bagha Singhs, it caused Saria's death, and everyone knows what happened to Mangaraj. Consider what befell Mangaraj's family after he took possession of it, before even six months and six fortnights had passed.

Four days after Mangaraj was arrested and taken to Cuttack, it was discovered that four knee-deep holes had been dug in the floor of his storehouse. The same day, it was learned that Gobinda and Champa were missing. Some people in the village reported that they had seen the two, walking one behind the other, in the low-lying fields of Padampur, along the Cuttack Road. Earlier, Mangaraj's sons had not been able to do as they liked for fear of displeasing their father, but this was a wonderful time for them. The eldest had always been a little crazy, and now he smoked so much cannabis that he went completely mad. The two younger sons were so busy these days that they did not have time to wipe their noses: since the Makara festival was drawing very close, they were busy trapping Gobara birds for the bird fights. Day and night, they sold off rice from the granary.

Today the village was astir with the news that Mangaraj's property would be put up for auction. It was about midday. A ja-madar, with a few constables and chowkidars—about eight to ten people—arrived at Mangaraj's doorstep. The judge Sahib had imposed a fine of one thousand rupees on Mangaraj; this money was going to be realized by auctioning off all his moveable property. The jamadar went inside and had all the articles brought out into the front yard. Mangaraj's daughters-in-law and the other women in the house left in fear, and gathered in the grove behind the house. They cried out of grief and confusion, just as Bani birds chatter in fear when a dhamana snake comes into their nest. Mangaraj's sons were nowhere to be seen. His record keeper was about to say something, but when the jamadar glared at him he sat down quietly on the verandah, his hand on his cheek.

Mukunda, the old farmhand, ran about in confusion, repeating, "Yes Sir, Yes Sir," to whatever was said.

The property was auctioned off, and what an auction it was! A pair of young bullocks, under the yoke for only two years, sold for four or five rupees. Had anyone ever heard of such a thing? The milk cows went for one rupee each, and two-year-old calves were given away for good measure. At the beginning people from Mangaraj's village did not bid for anything, but when they saw the prices were so low they began bidding against each other. The jamadar collected the money for the fine from the auction, and left. The cows and bullocks left unsold strayed into the fields; there was no one to take care of them. A few were taken away by cowherds from Bengal, and a few wandered off into neighboring villages. The farmhands had not received their dues for two full years; they now collected them by taking whatever they could from Mangaraj's groves, coconut gardens, and cowshed.

It was already the middle of the month of Kartika, but Mangaraj's corn still had not been harvested. The Pana farmhands had all run away; but they had not left empty-handed: they took cows and bullocks with them.

A small piece of news in a village gets exaggerated a thousand times when it reaches the marketplace. It was rumored everywhere that the judge Sahib had taken away Mangaraj's zamindari and given it to a lawyer, and that this lawyer would come with ten palanquins followed by five horses and two hundred foot soldiers to take possession of it on the next Makara Sankranti. On hearing this, the people of the village reminded one another, "Oh, horse, what difference does it make to you if you are stolen by a thief? You do not get much to eat here; you will not get much to eat there. No matter who becomes the next master, we will remain his slaves. We must look after our own interests."

Now, all Mangaraj's enemies were very happy. For fear and for shame, his henchmen could not show their faces in the village; how could they dare collect taxes? Addressing trees and bushes, mischievous villagers made caustic remarks at their expense.

CHAPTER TWENTY-SIX

Lalita Das, the Monk

The village of Gobindapur has been all astir since yesterday. Wherever you go—the marketplace, the bathing ghats, the cooking place, the places where rice is pounded—you hear the same story. Sometimes people speak in whispers, at others, loudly. One bigmouth is saying something, waving his hands about, and shaking his head. Five people are listening to him in rapt attention. The story has taken on various shapes. We will briefly summarize it here for you.

A monk from Puri arrived in Gobindapur seven days after Mangaraj was taken to Cuttack, and he made the Bhagavata room his resting place. Middle-aged and dark-complexioned, he was called Lalita Das. From the middle of his shaven head hung a tuft of hair, like the stem of a watermelon. As many as five necklaces of tulsi beads adorned his neck. Very early in the morning, he would get up, take his bath, and draw a line of sandal paste from the middle of his nose to the tuft of hair on his head. Then he would decorate his whole body with holy patterns in sandal paste and look like a postage-due letter from the dead-letter office, marked all over with official seals. After all this, he would go into the village to make speeches on the glory of Lord Hari. He wore only a loin cloth, no other outer garments. The name of Lord Hari was written all over his back, and in his hands he carried a cloth bag. During the day he moved about the village singing of Lord Hari; in the evening he performed kirtan, playing a khanjani. After this, he would read out the story of Chaitanya. In the evening, there would be a large gathering in the Bhagavataghara. Ten- or twelve-year-old weavers had already been initiated into the holy order to which the monk belonged. He was entirely free from greed, chanting, "Hare Kesta, Hare Kesta," whenever anyone gave him an offering. No one had ever seen such a great soul anywhere.

The monk had not been seen for two days now; he seemed to have vanished. People were also searching for Marua, the maid-servant in Mangaraj's house. Some were of the opinion that she had left for Brindaban in the company of the monk. If it was true she had joined the monk on a pilgrimage to this holy place, we must not cast aspersions on the character of holy men and women, or else we will be damned forever. However, one bit of news has made us feel somewhat uneasy. Marua was very close to Mangaraj's youngest daughter-in-law; she was always to be found near her young mistress. Now, along with Marua, the daughter-in-law's ornaments had also disappeared. In the box containing them there had also been the money that the daughter-in-law had received from her father and her father-in-law at the time of her marriage. Now it lay open, empty. Everyone made a connection between the disappearance of Marua and that of the ornaments and the money: the daughter-in-law howled in distress;

the other women of the house cried bitterly too, and after a time became quiet. There was no one to go after Marua.

The house, which had been crowded with people day and night, now looked utterly deserted. Grass overgrew the yards.

In a nutshell, within a matter of months, the power, prestige, and property of Mangaraj had all been scattered to the winds. It is said,

Nirjagāma yadā lakṣmīr
gajabhuktakapitthavat

When Lakshmi, the goddess of wealth, leaves a house,
It becomes like a kaintha fruit eaten by an elephant: an empty shell. *

---

*An old saying, and the translation is accurate. The image of the empty shell is meant to reveal the hollowness of the obsession with material prosperity.

CHAPTER TWENTY-SEVEN

A Marvelous Encounter

No one can escape his karma; you will suffer or prosper accordingly. No one can see a seed in the soil, but who can fail to notice it once it grows into a large tree? You may think yourself very clever, and you may imagine that no one can see what you do out of sight and in secrecy, but you will taste the fruits of the tree you have planted. And if you somehow escape, your successors will not. You are very proud of your might and your wealth, but you never know how someone you think is weak and insignificant can astonish you by his deeds. Even the subedar of Bengal, Bihar, and Orissa could not escape the consequences of torturing an ordinary fakir. And Sikh Guru Gobind Singh was able to save his life because earlier he had done a small favor to an ordinary Muslim. Leaving aside these grand historical events, consider how circumstances led Mangaraj to be tortured and humiliated by the Doms of Ratanpur, who had been sent to jail through his machinations because they were chowkidars for the Bagha Singh family.

When Mangaraj first arrived in jail the Doms of Ratanpur greeted him sarcastically, saying, "Our dear friend has come, our father-in-law has come, the great Saant has come," and then burst into peals of mocking laughter. When a wealthy person finds himself in jail, the leaders of the convicts harass him in the hope of extracting something. Whenever Mangaraj worked the oil press with the Doms, they landed blows on his back and face, and kicked him.

We had forgotten to mention that Gobara Jena, the chowkidar, had been sentenced to a year of rigorous imprisonment for giving false witness.

Time waits for no man; for eternity, day and night have followed each other at the same pace. Time would not stop for a while, just because Mangaraj was now working the oil press in jail. People say that happy days gallop like horses, and bad days walk like elephants. Whatever you may say, time knows how to do its job; it does not waste even a minute in a day. One, two, three, four . . . Days had gone by like this, and Mangaraj had completed two months of his prison term. One day, he had to be shifted to a different cell, since his needed repairs. There were eight earthen platforms in every cell; eight inmates spread their blankets on these to sleep. It so happened that the six Doms of Ratanpur, Gobara Jena, and Mangaraj were put into the same cell together.

Well, four days ago something terrible happened to Mangaraj. Since lunatic asylums such as the one in Dargha Bazaar in Cuttack did not exist in those days, lunatics had to be kept in jails. Their cell was only a short distance from Mangaraj's, and a very dangerous lunatic was kept there. He never slept at night, but danced wildly and shouted, "Oh, my Saria, oh, my six and a third acres." He jumped about, screamed, and laughed hysterically. Whenever he caught sight of Mangaraj, he lunged at him and tried to bite him. Every time he did so, the constables held him back. Four days ago, however, he suddenly broke free, charged at Mangaraj, and bit off part of his nose.

Today there was great commotion inside the jail: two severely injured prisoners were laid out in the yard. One was in his death throes, and he died soon after. The other was being cleaned and bandaged by the native doctor and his compounder. At about nine o'clock in the morning, the doctor Sahib arrived to see the body. He closely examined all parts of it. The jail daroga consulted the register and said, "This is the body of Gobara Jena, prisoner no. 977."

The injured prisoner who lay beside Gobara Jena was prisoner no. 957, Ramachandra Mangaraj. His body was swollen all over; the bridge of his nose was broken, and it was bleeding. From time to time, he vomited blood. The doctor Sahib decided that these symptoms indicated that the man had received a violent beating.

The matter was inquired into with great seriousness. There was a lot of running around, but it could not be ascertained who had done it. The man himself was not in a condition to say anything. Only the constable on guard duty said that he had heard sounds of someone pounding in the cell at midnight. The six Doms of Ratanpur submitted that the two inmates, Mangaraj and Gobara Jena, had had a terrible fight.

The inquiry was closed. The doctor Sahib declared the chances of the patient's survival to be bleak, and that the patient's friends and relatives should be permitted to take him home for treatment, if they so wished. The doctor Sahib's declaration was duly conveyed to Gobindapur by the police.

Mangaraj's sons had sold off all the grain, and the granary was now empty. They knew their father well; they knew they would get nothing if he returned from jail. And why should clever people like them knowingly take a risk? It is rightly said, "One should always look after one's own interests."

Mukunda, the old farmhand, in desperation, sold off two calves and a few cushions, and used the money to hire a palanquin and head for Cuttack.

The End

Mangaraj lay on the verandah near the sacred tulsi square, on an old mat, his head toward the north. Three months ago, Saantani had lain in exactly the same spot, in the same manner. His limbs were motionless, and his eyes stared unblinkingly at the sky. Two vaidyas, traditional healers, Siba Chamar and Kartik Nayak, attended to him, but last night they finally gave up and left, declaring his case beyond hope. Gopia, the weaver, alias Kaviraj Gopi, was a famous vaidya. He was highly regarded in the four neighboring villages, and was so busy he hardly ever found time to even wipe his nose. He would get up early in the morning, tie a shawl tightly around his waist, throw a red towel across his shoulder, and sling the small medicine bag from his arm. Carrying a bamboo staff, he would then go out to see his patients. Inside the bag, there were cure-alls for diseases and a piece of silk cloth containing several kinds of tablets. Gopi's uncle had also been a famous vaidya. Like pieces of flint, his medicines produced sparks of life in his patients. To this day, Gopi had preserved tablets prepared by his uncle.

Gopi sat at Mangaraj's right and felt his pulse for a long time. He looked up, closed his eyes, and bared his teeth. Mukunda kept gaping at the kaviraj's face. He asked, "Oh, kaviraj, what do you think?" The kaviraj became grave and replied, "It is said, 'Kanthaśleṣaprāṇāvinijāne kim punar dūrasamsthe.'"* In other words, it is dangerous if phlegm collects in the throat, and I shudder to think what will happen if it goes further down. But do not think I am an unlettered kaviraj like the others. Wait and see how I will drive the illness out; I will tie it in a knot and carry it away." Saying this he tied a knot in his cloth.

Mukunda asked why there was a swelling on the patient's body. Kaviraj observed, "It is said 'Svarṇadad tagunam sottham.' In other words, swelling is caused by phlegm. But do not worry, it will disappear as soon as a bit of musk reaches the patient's stomach. The patient should swallow a bit of musk and wear another as a mark on his forehead." The kaviraj took four annas from Mukunda and gave him a pinch of musk, to be taken with some other liquid. The kaviraj pronounced, "It is said 'Muṣṭakam kuttaki rātrī suntham pippalam eva ca.' In other words, at night, pound herbs such as sunthi pippali and bacha with a clenched fist." Mukunda asked, "How much of each shall I fetch?" "It is said, 'Anupānam vy eṣam karoti vividhān guṇān.' In other words,

---

*From Kalidasa's *Meghadutum:* "When the lover sees the clouds in the sky, he desires to throw his arms around the neck of his beloved. Since she is not near him, he suffers." The context in which this is uttered, with the kaviraj's pompous use of it to literally describe medical symptoms, suggests obvious incongruities, as well as the kaviraj's intention to deceive. (All Sanskrit quotations that follow are in fact garbled versions of Ayurvedic texts.)

if you give a patient a lot of liquid with these ingredients, it will strike a deadly blow against the disease."

While the kaviraj was busy discoursing on the nature of the disease and suggesting suitable remedies, the patient became restless. His breath failed, and from the corners of his eyes, tears rolled down his cheeks. Mangaraj had been suffering for four days now. All this time, he had been staring unblinkingly up into the sky. If he drifted off to sleep for a minute, he would wake up with a start and mutter in terror, "Six —— Th— Ac— . . ." His voice was feeble, and it grew weaker. Nothing he uttered could be heard clearly. Sometimes in his sleep, he saw a terrifying figure in the sky with long hair hanging loose from its monstrous head. Its white teeth looked like long thick turnips, and its tongue, two or three feet in length, lolled. It was rapidly advancing toward him to devour him. Mangaraj remembered that he had once seen a woman working the spindles on the verandah of the weaver's house. It seemed to be the same woman, who had now assumed this monstrous form and looked so grotesque and fearsome. And this terrifying figure thundered at him, "Give me my six and a third acres." In terror Mangaraj woke up, muttering, "Six —— Th— Ac— . . ." He drifted back to sleep and saw looming on the horizon the horrifying skeleton of a human with its jaws wide open, watching him intently, waiting silently to devour him. Mangaraj was certain that it was no one other than the woman who had starved herself to death in front of his house, because he had taken away her land. He also saw thousands of lunatics like Bhagia the weaver come rushing out of black clouds in the sky, holding swords and iron clubs. He felt as if all these clubs were raining down on his head. Mangaraj wanted to scream and run away; but he could not utter a word, and he felt too weak to move. Feeling utterly helpless, he turned his thoughts in heartfelt ardor to the one who protected the unprotected and redeemed the fallen. And then he saw the consoling vision of a woman, full of light, seated on a jeweled throne far above the circle of the sun in the endless sky. In times past, a lady used to sit beside Mangaraj's sickbed and comfort him by passing her hand over his limbs. This brilliant and beauteous figure of a woman seated on the jeweled throne was an image of this lady. She beckoned to Mangaraj. His soul left his mortal frame and flew toward her. The house swelled to chants of the Lord's name: "Haribol, Haribol, Haribol."

GLOSSARY

Prepared by Santosh Kumar Padhy

Alankar Shastra   The second-century A.D. (?) classical treatise on poetics, by the sage Bharata.

atoo   A ceiling made of mud and bamboo, below the thatch of a house, for storing things on top of it or to preserve things inside the house in case the thatch catches fire.

badi pala   Competition between two or more rival parties of Pala dancers. A Pala is a traditional dance-drama form of Orissa, in which a singer tells a story, embellishing it with references to and quotations from classical Oriya and Sanskrit literature.

baishnava   Worshipper of Lord Vishnu.

baksheesh   A tip.

Bhagavataghara   The room or house in an Oriya village where the *Bhagavata* (Jagannath Das's sixteenth-century Oriya translation) was read and discussed. A Bhagavataghara (also called a Bhagavatatungi) has for centuries been one of the main social and intellectual centers of most villages in Orissa, especially those with sizeable Hindu populations.

bhang Indian hemp, whose dried leaves, seeds, and small stalks are smoked, chewed, or pounded with black pepper and other spices for drinking in an infusion as a narcotic or hallucinogenic drug.

bharanas A local measure of grain, varying in different parts of Orissa.

Brahmos A reformist sect of Hinduism, originating in the nineteenth century.

chaprassis Peons.

chowkidar A village guard.

dacoits Bandits.

darshan An occasion on which one is permitted to see a god or an important person.

debottara Land given free of rent to defray the cost of worshipping a deity.

durbar Court.

Garuda A mythological bird, the carrier of Lord Vishnu.

jamadar Head constable.

kahali A small smoking pipe, usually of clay.

kajal Collyrium.

kanugoi A subordinate native revenue officer in the department responsible for land settlement.

kaviraj An Ayurvedic doctor.

kos A measure of distance, approximately two kilometers.

lakh One hundred thousand.

Makara Sankranti Summer solstice.

Marshman J. C. Marshman was a British missionary who arrived in Serampore in the 1820s. Working in close collaboration with William Carey, he wrote on historical matters relating to India and translated the Bible into Indian languages.

maund	A local measure, equivalent to forty kilograms.
munshi	Official doing the work of a secretary.
nabanna	A festival after harvest.
nautch girl	A dancing girl. *Nautch* is the Anglo-Indian rendering of *naatch*, the Hindi word for "dance."
noutis	A local measure of grain, varying in different parts of Orissa.
pajjhati	A traditional metrical scheme used in Sanskrit poetry.
pana	One of the many disadvantaged castes.
peshkar	A bench-clerk, formerly the person next in authority to the registrar in a court of law. A deputy *sheristadar.*
prasad	Food offerings to the temple god, afterward shared among the devotees.
pucca	Made with concrete and cement (as opposed to clay).
puja	Hindu ritual worship.
pulau	A dish, considered a delicacy, of rice cooked with meat or vegetables.
Saantani	Wife of the master of the house, expected to play the role of confidant and friend of the extended family and community.
Sadhaba	A Hindu woman whose husband is alive.
salagram	Stone worshipped as a symbol of Lord Vishnu.
sankirtan	An assembly for the purpose of group singing or chanting of *bhajans* (hymns) or devotional folk songs.
Shastra	"Text" or "treatise" (usually classical), either oral or written.
sloka	A short Sanskrit verse, used for ritual chanting or for traditional pedagogical purposes.
subedar	Formerly, an officer in charge of a province.
tanpura	A droning musical instrument with four metal

strings played as an accompaniment to a singer or another main musical instrument.

thana daroga   A police officer in charge of a police station called a *thana*.

Tod   Lt.-Col. James Tod, British political official in India, who wrote *Annals and Antiquities of Rajast'han, or the Central and Western Rajpoot States of India* (London: Smith, Elder, 1829–32).

ukhuda   Puffed rice coated with molasses; a delicacy usually offered to the gods.

Upendra Bhanja   Eighteenth-century Oriya poet who wrote in the ornate tradition of classical Sanskrit poetry.

ustad   Maestro.

Valmiki   A sage, author of the *Ramayana* in Sanskrit.

Text: 10/15 Janson
Display: Janson
Compositor: Bookmatters, Berkeley
Printer and binder: Integrated Book Technology